INFINITE LOVE

ELITE MEN OF MANHATTAN BOOK 6 NOVELLA

MISSY WALKER

This book is for you, the fans.
Thank you for wholeheartedly loving the Elite Men and
embracing their story.
The series will live on because of you.

1

BARRETT

It had been almost three years since I said "I do" to Lourde Diamond. Back then, I had no idea life could be this incredible. Now, we were the proud parents of little Colton, and I couldn't begin to describe how much love I have for that little guy.

Sinking back against the jet's leather seat, I released a soft, weary sigh that I hoped my wife didn't hear. I was too young of a man to feel so tired, but then there weren't many things quite like an active two-year-old, either. Colton could drain the energy from a fully charged battery if he set his mind to it.

It wasn't that I thought Lourde would worry about me—just the opposite. I was waiting for her to tease me about being unable to keep up. Though I knew it would be gentle and loving—she always was. My pride wouldn't allow for it.

But I'd be damned if the kid wasn't determined to wear us both down before Ari and Olivia said their vows.

"Colton." Lourde's voice was stern as she took hold of our son and returned him firmly to the seat next to her, facing mine. "What did I tell you? You have to keep your seat belt on when we're taking off. It's the *rule.*" That was the magic word. He was at an age where testing boundaries was always the order of the day, but whenever we brought up a rule—something that couldn't be broken—he fell in line.

I had to wonder how much longer that would last, but it was Lourde's opinion that we should enjoy it while we could. Eventually, he would be enough to know some rules could be bent if not broken. Considering his genes and the fact that neither of his parents ever cared much for rules, it seemed inevitable that we were in for it.

When Colton looked my way, I winked at him, and he gave me a tiny grin. "Listen to your mother," I said, and Lourde laughed softly.

"Why is it all you have to do is say *"listen to your mother,"* and he changes his tune?" she whispered, a little exasperated.

Now, Colton was happy to look at a picture book, gently kicking his feet as he flipped the pages. It had been a big day full of last-minute arrangements and packing extra clothing in light of a possible storm set to bear down on East Hampton on the day of the wedding. Lourde was nothing if not constantly prepared for any possibility. Now was the time for all three of us to wind down.

I didn't have an answer for her, so I could only shrug before returning to a couple of emails that needed my attention. We'd be spending the better part of a week in the Hamptons for Ari and Olivia's wedding, and while I wanted to step away from work for a while, there were a few issues that needed my attention before I could shut my brain off and focus on the time spent with my best friends.

"Just think," Lourde told Colton, brushing thick, chocolate-brown hair from his forehead as she spoke. "Noah will be there. You guys will have so much fun together this week." My heart swelled at the excitement on my son's face and the way he clapped his hands in anticipation of time spent with his own best friend. Ari and Olivia's son was a few months younger than Colton, but they were already joined at the hip. It was great to see, of course, and not a play date went by when Lourde didn't come home imagining the two of them being best friends for the rest of their lives. "Just like you and the other hunk holes," she would say.

Just like me and the other hunk holes. I laughed but hoped that was true. I wanted my son to be fortunate enough to find friends who would be by his side his entire life through all the ups and downs—changes like starting families and being responsible for more than just ourselves and our businesses.

"Sometimes I still can't believe it," I mused, chuckling softly while my phone sat untouched in my lap. I couldn't seem to get my thoughts together, not with memories overlapping and clouding my concentration.

Lourde looked up at me, and the sunshine streaming in through the window at her right highlighted the familiar curves of her perfect face. I had memorized them all during our time together, but she still never failed to captivate me. "Can't believe what?" she asked as a fond smile touched the corners of her mouth.

"Any of it. Another wedding. All of us settling down, having kids." I could only shake my head and laugh at myself when I remembered the not-so-distant past. The way my friends and I had torn through most of Manhattan's fuckable women without a second thought. "I never imagined this."

Her eyes lit up, reminding me so much of Colton. There was a moment when I couldn't breathe. He had her eyes, her nose, and the shape of her mouth. Lucky kid. "Maybe that's something you can use for your speech at the reception," she suggested. "You were saying you weren't sure what to talk about, right?"

She had a point. It wasn't the public speaking that bothered me. Normally, when the best man gave a speech at a wedding, it was filled with memories of times they'd shared, but I couldn't share many memories that would be appreciated in mixed company. We didn't need anybody gasping and clutching their vintage pearls.

As it was, Ari's grandmother was getting over being ill—it was still up in the air whether she would be able to attend the wedding, something that weighed heavily on Ari's mind. I didn't want to be responsible for her relapse because I shared details of past fun her grandson had gotten up to in our single days. She was a tough lady, formidable, but everybody had their limits.

Once we were in the air, and it was clear Colton couldn't stand sitting still a minute longer, Lourde unbuckled him so he could play with Naomi, his nanny. "Get him nice and tired out," I suggested, and I was only partly joking. While Naomi's presence meant we wouldn't have to worry about Colton while we took care of wedding business, I would still feel better knowing he was too exhausted to get up to mischief and run his nanny ragged. Lourde and I agreed she was a godsend, but never more than at a time like this.

"I'm so excited to finally see Olivia's dress." As Lourde spoke, her thumbs flew over her phone. "She just picked it up."

"Have you been able to get in touch with your brother? He's been MIA for the past few days."

Her thumbs went still, and her brow furrowed like she was thinking back before she shook her head. "Now that you mention it, no. I mean, I know they're coming, of course." Still frowning, she looked down at her phone and started typing another message. "What am I saying? The times I've reached out to Pepper, she's been vaguely busy too."

Interesting. After finishing my last email, I let my thoughts wander to my brother-in-law and his fiancée. "You don't think there's any trouble with them, do you?" I asked, waving off the offer of champagne from the attendant.

Lourde did the same, though she requested bottled water and fresh fruit for her and Colton. "No way. Not with them. And it's not like Pepper wouldn't tell me," she added with what I sensed was forced confidence.

"Then again, she might not since it's your brother she's engaged to," I pointed out.

"In two years, there's not much she hasn't told me." Her mouth tightened into a thin, almost disgusted frown. "Sometimes I wish she would keep certain things to herself. I'm not a prude, but he's still my brother."

"No, you are definitely not a prude." Now, as we flew over Long Island on our way to Ari's home, I couldn't help admiring my wife's firm legs. The soft, light sundress she wore meant getting a peek of her thighs whenever she moved or when the breeze hit her the right way and lifted the fabric.

She cleared her throat sharply, and I managed to pry my attention away from her legs to meet her gaze. "What, you're not satisfied after what I gave you this morning?" she asked, arching an eyebrow while delivering a knowing smirk.

"That was this morning," I pointed out with a growl. "Don't act like you don't love knowing I'm craving you again."

Her smirk faded, replaced by worry lines between her

delicately arched brows. "I'm a little concerned about Connor and Pepper. They would tell us if they were having problems, wouldn't they?"

"For one thing, they're not going to have problems. Not them." I knew Connor in a way his sister didn't and never would. I knew what it meant to have his perfect partner by his side. How it had changed him, the way I'd been changed. A man didn't simply let that slip through his fingers.

Lourde remained unconvinced. "They've been engaged all this time, though, without setting a date or even talking about it. And I know..." She chewed her lip while her eyes darted away, her attention directed out the window.

"There's nothing but clouds down there," I reminded her.

"No kidding," she retorted. "Maybe I like to look at clouds."

Maybe she liked changing the subject a little more. "Very funny. What were you going to say before you cut yourself off?" I pressed.

"Colton, settle down," Lourde said instead, craning her neck to look at our rambunctious son, who had apparently decided it would be fun to run races with himself up and down the aisle between the two rows of seats.

I'd told Naomi to wear him out, hadn't I? Perhaps not the best advice, considering where we were at the moment.

"Keep changing the subject." I sat back, folding my hands over my stomach and arching an eyebrow. "I can wait. I have nowhere else to be."

She only rolled her eyes at my joke. "I'm just saying, maybe there's a reason they've been engaged all this time but still haven't set a date. Maybe things aren't as strong as we want to think they are." Her teeth sank into her lip again, and those worry lines appeared. "I would hate that for both of them."

Moments like this reminded me of what drew me to her in the first place. All right, so her body and my unending hunger for it had played a part, but that wasn't enough to make a man jump through the sort of hoops I had jumped through to keep us together. My best friend sure as hell hadn't wanted me to be with his sister, and neither had her father at first. There were plenty of obstacles in our way, but nothing insurmountable. You don't go through what we did for the sake of a hot fuck.

Switching seats, I settled in next to my wife and took one of her hands in mine, which meant she had to stop picking nervously at the hem of her dress. "Dollface, look at me."

She complied, albeit in her own time, almost begrudgingly. "I would just hate for them to be having problems, especially with the wedding and everything over the next few days. Can you imagine us being in a bad place together and having to watch people you love get married and be blissfully happy?"

No. I couldn't. I didn't want to consider the idea since it would've meant considering the two of us being in a bad place. Nothing could've been further from the truth. We had been on a two-year honeymoon, and nothing would change that.

"Do you want to know one of the things I love most about you?" I laced my fingers through hers, locking our hands together. "Your heart. You love so hard. You also worry just as hard, and I know Connor wouldn't want that."

Her chin trembled slightly before she caught herself, then sighed. "He's my brother. She's my best friend."

"And sometimes, we have to trust people," I reminded her as gently as I could. "We must believe if they need our help and are going through a hard time, they'll come to us. Right?"

"That's true, I guess." However, she didn't seem convinced, not by a long shot. "I'm probably being overly emotional."

"Well, there's a big event in front of us. You know you always get emotional around weddings." Another thing to love about her, along with so many others. "Don't try to put out a fire we don't know is burning. One thing at a time."

"Right, of course." She gave her body a little shake as if trying to brush off her worries, which naturally made all of the appetizing parts of her shake temptingly enough to grab my dick's attention.

"You'd better be careful about that," I warned, making sure we weren't being watched before letting my free hand roam beneath her hem. "I might not be able to help myself."

Her cheeks flushed, and she giggled. "Don't even give me the spiel about the Mile High Club because we're already card-carrying members."

She didn't have to tell me that. The fact was, it didn't matter if we were miles in the air, in the back of the car, or sneaking a quickie in the pantry while Colton was taking a nap. We tended to christen just about every location we happened to visit. There was no quenching my thirst for her body, for the blissful oblivion that came with sinking deep into her and letting go of everything else in favor of what only she could give me.

For the time being, I settled for indulging in her silky thigh before behaving like a good boy and leaving my hand in my lap. "This is going to be a great event. I want you to relax and enjoy yourself. Do all the wedding things you've been talking about for weeks. Don't worry so much. They'll let us know if there is a problem, and then we can try to help them. All right?"

I didn't quite believe her sunny smile, but I pretended to. "Right. This is about Ari and Olivia. Everything's going to be great," she chirped.

Just the same, as we were preparing to land and Colton was strapped into his seat again, I shot Connor a quick text.

Me: *Will be at the airport in a few minutes. Looking forward to seeing you two there.*

By the time we landed and were waiting for our luggage to be loaded into the waiting limo, I hadn't received a reply. Lourde's concerns rang out in my head, though I pretended otherwise for her sake. My best friend would tell me if something was wrong. Wouldn't he?

2

BARRETT

"I want to see Noah!" Colton's feet swung wildly, kicking the seat as the limousine traveled the short distance from the East Hampton Airport to Ari's estate.

"Kicking the seat won't get us there any faster," I reminded him.

Lourde had a point. There were times when all it took was a sharp tone from me to stop him dead in his tracks.

"Somebody's feeling rammy today." Lourde managed to say it with nothing but love hanging in her words. Motherhood fit her like a glove.

She was endlessly patient, which I could admit also helped in our relationship. I wasn't always the easiest to love, and I knew it, but she made it look effortless.

"Noah will be there," she explained for maybe the hundredth time. "And your cousins. Don't forget about them."

I was barely able to stifle a laugh when Colton sighed dramatically. "You'd think he pays his own bills," I murmured, making Lourde giggle behind her hand.

"Babies!" Colton insisted. It wasn't the time to remind him that Magnus and Evelyn's twin girls weren't much younger than him. He wouldn't understand, anyway.

"But they're still your cousins, so try to play nice," I reminded him while we passed one mansion after another as we approached the village, after which we would reach the sprawling estate where the wedding would take place.

"It will be good to see Evelyn," Lourde murmured while scrolling through the list of activities scheduled for the wedding party and select guests in the days before the ceremony. "She's been so busy lately."

She dropped the phone into her Birkin before leaning against me. I smiled to myself, thinking back on the years my sister felt directionless, cut off from the world thanks to her injured leg and the years of psychological abuse that had led to the day of her injury. I might have paid for her surgeries and the therapy that followed, but I wasn't arrogant enough to believe that did the trick of pulling her out of her shell. Not completely. It had been Magnus who'd brought her to life.

When I looked back on how absolutely fucking furious I had been when the two of them got together, it was enough to make me ashamed of myself. Not only had I acted like a hypocrite since Connor was ready to murder me for being with his sister in the beginning, but I'd also underestimated Magnus. He had been nothing but good for Evelyn, and the confidence she'd gained had given her the strength to open a nonprofit aimed at helping women with disabilities find work and a sense of purpose, which she had gone without for so long.

"It will be good to have a chance to catch up with everyone," I agreed, brushing my lips over the top of her head.

She looked up at me and smiled before delivering a brief but loving kiss.

Colton squealed. "Kiss Colton! Kiss Colton!" There was nothing for Lourde to do but helplessly laugh as she obeyed our son's wishes.

"Just as demanding as your daddy," she joked before giving him a big, smacking kiss on his cheek.

"I don't hear you complaining," I murmured close to her ear when she settled back in, and she responded by swatting playfully at my arm. However, there was nothing playful in her eyes when they met mine. Suddenly, my most pressing priority was to get her alone as quickly as possible after we arrived.

"Oh, it's already so beautiful."

I followed the direction of Lourde's gaze as we approached the estate. The wedding wasn't scheduled to take place for another two days, but an event like this couldn't be pulled off overnight. Ari had gone all out, which was no surprise. He would spare nothing when it came to Olivia, a sentiment I could relate to.

As far as I was concerned, Lourde could have anything she wanted. Money was no object when it came to her happiness.

Multiple tents were being set up along the grounds, the longest I assumed was intended for the reception. Lights twinkled away in there, hundreds if not thousands strung overhead. Workers rolled tables inside, pulling them down from a large truck, while another truck full of chairs was being unloaded nearby. From the looks of them, they would be for the wedding ceremony, which was set to take place on a cliff overlooking the water where a large archway was in the process of being constructed.

The driver pulled into the circular courtyard in front of

the mansion, narrowly avoiding a panicked-looking young woman holding a tablet in one arm. "One of the wedding planners," Lourde guessed as the girl ran past. With the windows rolled up, it wasn't possible to hear what she was shouting, but she seemed fairly frantic as she hurried toward the workers.

A second girl greeted us once we stepped out of the limo. "Welcome," she said, wearing a bright smile. "You must be the Black family."

After a wave of her hand, a kid who looked barely old enough to shave jumped to attention and started gathering our bags. "Josh will take your things up to your assigned rooms," the girl explained in a bright but professional tone. "Mr. Goldsmith asked if you would join him on the back terrace when you arrived."

"Has anyone else arrived yet?" I asked while Lourde gave instructions to Naomi. As much as he wouldn't like the idea, it was time for Colton's nap. He would be a holy terror if he missed it.

"Mr. and Mrs. Miller have arrived," the girl replied after checking her tablet, referring to Magnus and Evelyn. "We're only waiting on Mr. Diamond and Ms. Little, but they're expected shortly." She then touched a hand to the earpiece she wore, giving us a respectful little nod before darting off to handle another task.

Connor and Pepper had yet to arrive. It didn't have to mean anything, though the furrowing of Lourde's brow told me she thought otherwise.

"We should go back and see them." Lourde took my hand as we climbed the stairs leading up to the sweeping front terrace bordered by an intricately carved stone parapet that had already been hung with lights and adorned with large planters dripping with luscious cream flowers.

"They can wait a minute." I hadn't spent almost an entire flight and limo ride ogling my wife's legs to head straight back to our friends. Rather than allow her to lead me along the flagstone terrace, I pulled her into the house and made a beeline for the closest powder room at the opposite end of the enormous, marble-floored entry hall. There were perks to knowing the mansion's layout after paying so many visits.

"What are you doing?" Lourde whispered, giggling uncontrollably by the time we reached the lavishly appointed room. I had been in walk-in closets smaller than where I'd retreated with my wife, who locked the door behind us despite her weak, ineffectual protests.

"Getting something out of my system in hopes of being able to concentrate on anything else for the rest of the day," I replied with a growl. Rather than wasting time with formalities, I pulled her close and worked my hands beneath her dress to cup her firm ass.

Her soft moan made my already hardening dick stiffen fully, and the touch of Lourde's hand against my covered erection was enough to make me ache painfully. "What's this?" she whispered, stroking my bulge while sliding her tongue against my lips.

I answered by thrusting my tongue into her mouth, swirling and probing until she whimpered and melted in my arms. The marble sink proved sturdy enough to support her once I placed her on its edge, nudging her thighs apart with my own.

"Barrett..." she whispered, a sound I would never get tired of. She had said my name that way more times than I could count, lost in bliss, giving herself over to me because I was the only one who could do this to her. There was magic between us.

The brush of my fingers between her legs left me

covering her mouth with mine to stifle her moans. She was already wet, so hot, and my single focus became getting to the center of that heat. Instinct demanded I push the patch of cotton aside rather than remove her thong.

She gasped at the presence of my fingers gliding through her wetness, her fingers twisting in my hair, holding my head in place while she kissed me. Claiming me as I claimed her, I was unable to control the scorching heat threatening to burn both of us to ashes.

I couldn't wait anymore. She helped with my belt and zipper, both of us breathing hard, panting for breath. Suddenly, nothing in life that mattered more than being inside her.

Yet she stopped me before I could line up with her dripping entrance. "Wait. Like this." She hopped off the sink and turned around, facing me in the mirror while she hiked her dress up to her waist and lowered the thong to her knees.

Just when I thought I couldn't love her more. Looking down, I watched my dick disappear inside her tight, hot sheath. Inch by inch, I worked my way in until I was flush against her firm ass, her satisfied moan leaving me struggling to hold back my explosion.

With one hand on the back of her neck, I bent her forward, her face close to the mirror. With my other hand on her hip, I took her hard and fast. "Oh, shit," she whispered, pushing back against me, meeting me stroke for stroke. Her eagerness only made everything hotter, more real, and more exciting. My heart raced, my blood pumped, and the sound of strangers working on the other side of the door heightened the thrill.

The sight of her bouncing tits reflected in the mirror was enough to make me salivate. My hand left her hip in favor of holding them, then lowered the front of the dress to expose them to my hungry gaze. "Ooh, yes," she moaned out when I played with her nipples, pushing back harder than before while her greedy cunt sucked me deeper. "Fuck me, Barrett."

"You're so hot," I grunted through clenched teeth, pounding her the way she needed. "Look at me. Watch me, Doll Face."

She opened her eyes and met my gaze in the mirror, flushed and breathless, tits bouncing, her lips parted so each short, stifled breath could slip through. It was like something out of a dirty fantasy, only there was nothing imaginary about this.

Mine. She was mine and always would be. We would spend the rest of our lives this way. No matter what was happening around us, we could come back to this. Us.

The clenching of her already tight sheath had me gritting my teeth. I was barely holding on, thanks to the combination of the feel of her pussy and the sight of her abandon in the mirror. "Come for me," I groaned out, our bodies slapping together in a desperate rhythm while the tension built until it was unbearable.

At the last second, I covered her mouth with my hand to catch the ecstatic cries she couldn't hold back. She shouted behind my palm, and I barely held back my groans while her pussy milked me dry.

Lourde could only get three words out. "Oh my God." She leaned over the sink, legs shaking, while the evidence of our quickie glistened on her thighs and shaved pussy. I held her in place with one hand and gently cleaned her using the other while she caught her breath. By the time I finished, she'd straightened up and got herself together.

"We should visit friends more often," I suggested before

kissing the back of her neck, adjusting my clothing as I did. "It's an aphrodisiac."

"Like you need one," she murmured before giggling. "We've done that at home too."

"Not with dozens of workers running around," I pointed out in a whisper, grinning when she rewarded me with a blush.

Her phone rang not a moment later, breaking the spell. "Finally. Maybe it's Pepper," she murmured as she pulled it free, then frowned. "Brad Morris. Why would he call me?"

Instantly, my hackles rose. "Who's he?" I demanded, ready to take the phone from her.

"You've met him a bunch of times. He works for *TMZ*." She shrugged when our eyes met. "It could be important."

I waved a hand, watching intently as she answered. "Brad? I'm sorry, I'm—"

Her excuse to get off the phone died, though the guy on the other end spoke quietly enough that I couldn't make out anything he said. It didn't quite matter. Not when Lourde's face fell further with every passing moment.

"This isn't good." The tremor in her voice paired with the anxiety shining in her wide eyes. I raised my brows expectantly, and she responded by turning on the phone's speaker so I could hear the other side of the call. "You're on speaker," she told Brad. "Barrett is here."

He didn't waste time with pleasantries. "Like I was saying..." he nearly whispered, "... *TMZ* got their hands on some photos of Connor partying in Vegas. They want to publish them but are going to wait until the drug den story loses traction before going live." I vaguely recalled hearing something about the latest surefire Oscar contender being discovered slinking out of a drug den within the past day or so. America's sweetheart got caught in the middle of a binge, and the press ate it up with a spoon.

"Partying?" I asked, exchanging a look with Lourde. "Do you have details? That could mean anything."

"Sorry I wasn't able to get my hands on anything else, but it sounds pretty wild," he murmured. "I shouldn't even be telling you this, but I figured I'd warn you. I'd say they'll be out in twenty-four hours, maybe forty-eight tops."

Thanks to the emotions washing over her face I could see Lourde playing out possible outcomes in her head. No doubt her father would have a fit, not to mention her mother. I might not have been raised with wealth, but I understood the importance of image. To them, image was everything, and the notion of Connor ruining the prestigious Diamond name by being involved in some drunken orgy in Las Vegas would set off a number of explosions.

"Thank you for the heads up," I managed to conclude before ending the call. I felt sick. Was it true? If so, how could he do it?

It seemed Lourde was reading my mind. "How could he?" she whispered, her jaw clenched. There were no tears in the question. No, in fact, she sounded angry more than anything. "I thought he was better than this."

"Let's not jump to conclusions," I urged, though I had already jumped to a few of my own. If he fucked this up, we would have words—very strong ones. Pepper was the best thing that ever happened to him, something I thought he knew.

"It would make sense, though," she insisted in a fierce whisper. "You said it yourself. He's been MIA for days. And I can't get a hold of Pepper, either. They're also not here yet. What if they broke up and that's why Pepper is MIA while he was out partying? And they didn't want to tell us because they didn't want to ruin things right before the wedding?"

"Then we'll deal with it." Really, it was the only conclusion to come to. "We'll know more when they arrive."

If they arrive.

It wasn't enough to calm her, not that I expected it to. "Would they say anything? Fuck, should I even tell Connor about the photos? I guess I should, right?"

I couldn't provide a quick answer to that. It would mean admitting we knew there was trouble, but sitting on it without at least giving Connor the heads up would be the same as betrayal. "I'll see if I can pull him aside," I decided, rubbing her arms before taking her face in my hands. "We'll keep it discreet. The most important thing is to make sure everything goes well for Olivia and Ari. Who knows? We might be able to silence the story. I'm sure *TMZ* has a price I could match."

"Maybe." Suddenly, her eyes flashed, and her nostrils flared. "I will drag him down to the beach and hold him underwater if he broke her heart, so help me."

I tried to be lighthearted as I pulled her in for a hug. "That's my girl... but you'd have to wait in line. Now, come on," I urged as warmly as possible, considering my growing anger with my idiot friend. "Let's shake this off, go out and see everybody, and we'll cross that bridge when we come to it."

3

———

BARRETT

"There you are! Chloe said you got here a little while ago." Olivia smiled brilliantly, coming our way with her arms spread wide once we emerged from the house. "We thought maybe you got lost."

After a brief hug, I turned to Ari, who wore an expression I recognized. Now that the big day loomed over him, he was overwhelmed, maybe even nervous. I'd felt similarly in the days leading up to my wedding. There wasn't a doubt in my mind I was making the right move. If anything, I would've married Lourde sooner, but there were things like reservations, florists, and shit like that to work out.

Still, there was something about the word forever and joining your life to somebody else's and being responsible for their happiness until your final breath. It was a big fucking deal and not something to take lightly.

"Not getting cold feet, are you?" I joked as we shook hands. "Does your best man need to make sure you don't make a run for it?"

"Knock that shit off," my sister warned. Evelyn rose from her chair, giving me a wry smirk before pairing it with a tight hug. After two years, there were still times when it surprised me to find her walking smoothly without the limp she'd struggled with for so many years. No one would ever guess there'd been a time when she felt isolated and small, not when she was so vibrant and outgoing after emerging from her cocoon.

Being her brother, I couldn't resist the impulse to annoy her. "I'm just making sure we don't have a runaway groom!" Magnus laughed loudly enough that his wife shot him a withering look that shut his mouth.

"Enough ball-busting," Olivia announced, her arm looped around Lourde's as she led us to the table beneath a large, striped umbrella. On it sat crudités, bruschetta, and other finger foods, which Lourde happily started to enjoy.

"I don't know how you do it with two kids at a time," she confessed to Evelyn around a mouthful of bruschetta on a slice of crostini. "I forgot to eat this morning. I was so busy making sure I had everything in place."

"You know, that's why Naomi is here," I reminded her before accepting a glass of scotch on the rocks from Ari. As I expected, my words fell on deaf ears. Lourde enjoyed being a hands-on mother and juggling her interior design business as much as I enjoyed running my empire.

Evelyn and Magnus shared a weary but loving glance. "We definitely rely on all the help we can get," Evelyn admitted with a soft laugh. "Between my hours at the nonprofit and the two of them growing like weeds and running around like crazy, there wouldn't be any handling it on our own."

"They're napping now," Magnus added before yawning loudly and making us all laugh.

"Maybe you could use a nap, old man," I suggested before taking a seat. The sun had broken through the clouds, now sparkling on the water which spread out before us. The air was sweet and balmy, and being with my friends made everything just about perfect.

One thing was missing. No, two things. Lourde glanced my way before asking, "So where are my idiot brother and his patient fiancée? He'll be late for his own funeral."

"No idea." Ari shrugged as he sat on my right with a scotch of his own. "I got a quick message from him last night saying they would see us today." Ari sounded unbothered, but then there was no reason for him not to.

Lourde shot another worried look my way before addressing the group. "Has he seemed okay lately?" Has anybody noticed anything off?"

"In what way?" Evelyn asked.

"Oh, I don't know." I watched as my wife did her best to play it off like there was nothing to worry about. It was a little too late for that, judging by the looks of concern everyone else wore. "Don't listen to me. Just worrying about my brother for no reason."

A brother who, as it turned out, was on his way across the terrace with an arm around Pepper's waist. "Your ears must be burning!" Olivia called out, waving an arm over her head. "We were just talking about you."

They both hesitated half a second before resuming their approach. "I don't know if I like the sound of that," Connor offered, removing his Ferragamo sunglasses and perching them on top of his head as he shot questioning looks at all of us.

"Just wondering where the hell you were." Lourde made it a point to jump up and hug her brother, effectively ending the topic. "You look too skinny," she decided, holding him at arm's length.

"Listen to her." Connor rolled his eyes at me before

chuckling. "She pops out a kid, and suddenly, she's everybody's mother." The gentle shove Lourde gave him made him laugh harder.

"Fine. See if I care. Wither away." Lourde sat on my lap to free up a chair for Pepper, who sank into it with a sigh.

"Traffic was a nightmare. We should have flown," she told Connor, who could only shrug. "Anyway, here we are. Hopefully, we didn't miss anything."

On the surface, everything seemed normal. Pepper still wore the engagement ring Connor had given her, and they sat almost as close to each other as Lourde and I did. Connor draped an arm around her shoulders as they settled back into their chairs, and Pepper reached up to take Connor's hand, resting on her shoulder—the sort of careless, intimate gesture born from years spent together.

What was I thinking? I was letting Lourde get in my head. Just because Connor went to Vegas didn't mean he was cheating on Pepper. All right, so I might have liked being invited on a guys' trip, but that wasn't grounds to declare their relationship null and void. "What have you been up to lately?" I asked Connor while Lourde loaded a plate with cheese, crackers, and meats from an elaborate tray. "You've been a ghost."

There it was. Connor's gaze shifted. One second, he was looking at me. The next, he was staring over my shoulder. "Oh, you know," he murmured, sounding vague. "I've been busy."

"Anything interesting?" Lourde prodded, and I was proud of how casual she managed to sound.

"You know how it goes," he told her with a chuckle. "Business, business, business. I have to keep reminding myself not to turn into a boring old prick like Dad."

"Don't worry." Pepper snuggled a little closer to him. "I won't let you. If you get boring, we're done."

"With all that work…" I mused, "… it's good for you to get away like this. When's the last time you got away for a little while?"

This time, Connor stared into his glass Ari had provided. "Oh, I don't know. I can't remember." He looked to his fiancée, who shrugged.

"No idea. We've both been so busy," she replied.

A general sense of unease tinged the breeze that stirred the fringe on the umbrella overhead. Something was off, and it was clear from the looks Evelyn and Magnus gave me that they felt it too.

Olivia clapped her hands, grabbing everyone's attention. "Okay, boys, I know none of you are interested in the finer points of wedding arrangements, so I'm going to take the girls inside to see my dress!"

Lourde was off my lap in a shot, bouncing up and down on the balls of her feet. "I can't wait!" she squealed, and soon the women scurried off, giggling and gushing over how wonderful everything was going to be.

I looked Ari's way in time to catch his loving grin as he watched them retreat. "That makes it all worth it," he murmured loud enough for only me to hear. "Watching her like that. All the questions from the planners, the scheduling conflicts, and the invoices. It's all good, so long as she's happy."

"Now, just keep that in mind for the next fifty years, and you're golden." I raised my glass to him, and he did the same.

In the back of my mind, I couldn't help but wonder when to pull Connor aside and ask what the hell he was trying to hide from us.

Magnus looked murderous, and the flickering glow from the bonfire heightened his stormy expression. "You're fucking kidding me. What an asshole move," he growled out.

I scowled and shook my head slightly, then looked across the fire to where Connor lounged on a blanket. He and Ari were deep in conversation about extra arrangements Ari had made to surprise Olivia. He was flying her favorite singer in just for the reception, and all the arrangements left him checking his phone seemingly nonstop.

"We still don't know for sure what it's all about," I reminded Magnus in a tight, hushed voice. "And we don't want to ruin anything. I'm not sure what to do. Do I reach out to *TMZ* and pay to kill the story? What if it's all over nothing?"

"They seem fine," Magnus pointed out. The girls were sitting together on the terrace, and their laughter floated our way on the evening breeze. They were already well into another pitcher of sangria from the sound of it.

"Do they, though? He's been weird all day. Sort of spacy," I observed, watching Connor talking with Ari. He seemed fine at the moment, but throughout the day, I'd caught him staring off and sometimes frowning like he had something on his mind that pissed him off.

"That's true," Magnus agreed, sounding disheartened. "He zoned out on me twice during dinner in the middle of a conversation."

"Lourde is beside herself." As if on cue, the familiar sound of my wife's laughter reached my ears. "Granted, I think the sangria is helping," I added, making Magnus laugh.

"I say we pull him aside," he decided. "We don't have to

make a big deal about it, but he needs to know what's coming. If those pictures come out and he's blindsided, I'll feel like shit. Even if he deserves it a little," he adds with a growl.

"We don't know that he did anything wrong," I reminded him.

"Fuck that. He deserves it for not inviting us." We shared another laugh that went a long way toward easing my tension. That was the thing about being with old friends, shooting the shit, talking about old times the way we had been all day. I could laugh despite the indecision playing tug-of-war in my head.

"Hey, you." The presence of a woman's sultry voice drew my attention, and I watched as Pepper bent down and wound her arms around Connor's neck. "There's something we need to discuss."

"Can we discuss it later?" he asked, but she only took him by the hand and began to tug until he finally relented and stood, brushing sand off his khakis.

"Don't worry, boys," Pepper purred, leading her man away with a swing in her hips. "I'll have him back to you in one piece before you know it." Meanwhile, the rest of the women whistled and laughed on the terrace.

It appeared we would have to wait to find out the story behind Connor's wild trip. One thing was for sure—things seemed perfectly fine between him and Pepper, and it was enough to give me hope that all of this was easily explained.

4

CONNOR

It was pointless to ask her what the big hurry was. I knew. That was why I didn't bother arguing. Besides, it was much more fun to stare at Pepper's swaying ass—round, ripe, like a juicy fruit begging for me to sink my teeth in.

Our time together hadn't cooled off my hunger for her. If anything, I wanted her more on that beach than I ever had. There was something especially tempting about her sexy, seductive attitude tonight.

"Where are we going?" I finally had to ask when I stumbled over a piece of wood that must have washed up on the beach. We were getting farther from the bonfire, and the darkness made it tough to see where I was going. It didn't help that I'd had a couple of drinks with the guys, and my head was foggy. Not foggy enough to lessen the raging erection now tenting my khakis, of course. It would take a hell of a lot more than a little scotch to do that.

"I've been dying to drag you away all night," she told me over her shoulder, her voice full of wicked promise. We were now approaching the rear of the property, and up ahead, I could barely make out the stairs leading from the mansion down to the boathouse. Everything had been strung up with lanterns for the reception, but they were dark now, swinging in the breeze.

"Watch your step," she warned as we entered the small structure. At the moment, everything was dark and quiet except for the gentle bobbing of a boat on the water coming in from the bay. Perfect for a little fun, in other words.

Once we were inside with the door closed, she was on me, or maybe I was on her. It didn't matter which of us attacked first, only that we were soon lost in a haze of hands and mouths, fumbling in the dark. I traced the familiar curves of her body—lush, firm, full—while she moaned into my mouth.

Then, because of the confidence she had gained and the fact she could never give up control for long, she grabbed my bottom lip and sucked before nipping it until I hissed. If anything, it made me want her more and heightened the heat between us. I dug my fingers into her ass and hauled her in to grind my cock against her. "Is this what you want?" I whispered against her throat before running my tongue over her skin. After spending hours sitting outside, she tasted like salty air, something that shouldn't have been sexy but worked with her warm skin and the wine still on her breath. "So hungry for my cock, you can't wait? You have to drag me away for a quick fuck?"

She answered with a throaty moan before cupping my bulge and giving it a gentle, tantalizing squeeze. "It's been too long since I had my hands on this."

I let out a laugh, but it was cut short when I slid my hand into the top of her dress, grabbing her breast. "We were late because we couldn't get out of bed earlier," I reminded her before pulling the front of the dress down so I could bury my face between her round, firm globes and lap at every inch of her skin.

"Suck on them." She almost forced me to lift my head and take a nipple between my lips, then loudly moaned when I flicked it with the tip of my tongue. "Oh fuck, just like that."

I backed her against the wall and gave her what she wanted, going back and forth, licking and sucking until the fingers she wound through my hair twisted, then pulled my head up so she could cover my mouth with hers. Caging her in with my arms, I kissed her hard, grinding my aching cock against her and stroking her tongue with mine. Her deep moans filled my ears, along with the pounding of my heart.

It wasn't enough. She had started this, but I was the one in control, the one sliding the dress up over her thighs and sinking to my knees. The familiar scent of her arousal was much stronger than scotch or any drug. It went straight to my head. Nothing but the taste of her sweet pussy would do now. I needed it more than oxygen.

"Mm... that's right." Her breathless whispers drove me on, making me work to get to the center of the heat radiating from her. "Lick my pussy. I need your tongue..."

Fuck me. I would never get tired of hearing her like that, demanding what she wanted as she spread her thighs, leaning her back against the wall so I could feast on her.

I shouldn't have been surprised when I found nothing but smooth, shaved skin, already glistening with her juices by the time I ran my tongue along her seam. "Bad girl," I growled out, inhaling her fragrant aroma. "Running around with no panties?"

"Less talking," she muttered, taking me by the back of the head with one hand, pressing my face closer, and grinding her hips until there was nothing for me to do but use my tongue to part her lips, delving through her swollen folds. I could've died there, between her thighs, and been happy about it. I wanted nothing more than this.

She moved her hips, riding my face, building up to what was going to be a shattering orgasm by the sound of her rasping breaths. "Oh... yes... yes, yes, more... I'm gonna come," she whimpered out through her pants for breath. I focused on her clit, lapping it wildly, and that was all it took for her back to arch and a long, throaty moan to fill the air.

My head was spinning by the time I stood, only for Pepper to take me by the shoulders and steer me to a bench a few feet away. I unzipped my pants and withdrew my aching dick, rock-hard and dripping with need for the woman who straddled me once I was seated.

No matter how almost painfully erect I was or how close I was to sinking deep into her, I had to take a second to soak in the moment—the woman in my lap the most perfect woman to walk the planet. She knew how to drive me crazy. She filled all the cracks in my life and fit with me like a puzzle piece.

She lifted herself off my thighs and wrapped her slim fingers around my shaft. Her touch made me suck in a sharp breath that turned to a satisfied groan once my swollen head broached her quivering entrance and stretched her tight muscles. "Fuuuck..." I grunted, letting my head fall back as she sank lower, swallowing me an inch at a time.

Taking my jaw in her hand, Pepper whispered, "God, I love you," before capturing my mouth with hers. Then she began to move, rising and falling in one slow, sensual stroke after another. I took hold of her ass, squeezing it, moving her up and down. There was nothing like it. I was a king when I was inside her.

When she broke the kiss to suck in a ragged breath, my

lips trailed down her throat and across her chest. "Yes!" She whimpered, moving faster when I sucked her nipple into my mouth while massaging her other tit. "Connor!"

I loved it when she said my name like that. Helpless, almost pleading, begging me for more. Her movements became shorter and faster until we were rutting like two animals while her tits bounced between us. I watched her lose herself, throwing her head back in abandon, her black curls a tangled mess before a high-pitched cry stirred in her throat in time with the clenching of her pussy.

"I'm coming! Oh, fuck!" She squealed, then shuddered, going limp against me while the muscles gripping my cock began to ripple. Heat slashed my core as I pumped her up and down once, twice, before I couldn't hold it any longer and let go. The rush was better than any I had ever known, but then everything about us was better than anything until she crashed into my world.

"What was that all about?" I asked once I caught my breath, stroking her soft curls as she rested her head on my shoulder. "Not that I'm complaining or anything. Don't get the wrong idea."

"I told you." She sat up, arms around my neck. My eyes had adjusted to the darkness long before then, and I could make out the sexy gleam in her eyes. "I couldn't wait to get my hands on your cock. Twelve hours is too long."

"Even when you're having a good time with your girls?" I teased as I kissed her cheeks, nose, and forehead until she giggled.

"I love my girls." She touched her forehead to mine before giggling again. "But, you know, there's certain things they just can't provide."

"They're going to know we were doing this out here." Not that I gave a shit. I had done much worse in much more public places. There was hardly a club bathroom in Manhattan I hadn't at least gotten a blowjob in over the years.

But that was over. It had been over from the moment things shifted between us. When we had first gone from acquaintances to much more, she'd wiped out the memory of every other woman who'd ever existed. In the blink of an eye, they had ceased to exist. She had become the center of my world.

Lifting a shoulder, she climbed off my lap and started pulling herself together. "They aren't exactly nuns themselves, you know," she reminded me. "We compare notes sometimes."

"Oh? You share all the dirty details?" It wasn't a surprise. I had heard women laughing together before when they were dishing over the private details of their lives, and that sort of laughter had floated down from the terrace earlier. Loud and bawdy.

"Please," she muttered with a smirk as I stood. "Like you guys don't talk about sex. Don't insult my intelligence."

I slipped an arm around her waist on the way out of the boathouse. The clouds that had covered the sky on and off throughout the day had broken, and now a three-quarter moon lit everything around us. The water sparkled almost as brightly as Pepper's eyes when she turned to me and wrapped her arms around my waist. I used my fingers to comb out a few of her dark curls before taking her face in my hands. "If there's one thing I can guarantee will never happen, it's losing sight of your intelligence for a single second." It was one of the things I loved best about her. She was sharp as hell, fiery. She kept me on my toes, and I loved every fucking second of it.

"So you aren't going to pretend you don't tell the hunk

holes about some of the crazy shit we get up to?" She arched an eyebrow while her full lips twitched.

"Not anymore, and that's the truth. Maybe back in the day," I admitted, feeling a little embarrassed by that old version of myself when the guys and I would exchange stories over drinks, tucked away in the back corner of countless clubs and bars. We'd done our best to one-up each other in those days, dropping the names of models and heiresses.

"Are you saying I reformed you?" she asked with a playful gasp, touching her chest and fluttering her eyelashes. "Is that what you're saying, Mr. Diamond?"

"That's what I'm saying... *Mrs.* Diamond." It still sounded strange but in a good way. I wore what was probably a goofy grin, though Pepper's radiant smile told me she didn't mind.

"Even though I don't know whether I'll change my name..." she said softly, standing on her tiptoes, "... I do like the sound of that." Her kiss was light and playful.

We started back along the beach, arms around each other, the bonfire in the near distance. The girls had come down to join their men, and now everyone laughed and shouted jokes across the fire. "Not the sort of honeymoon people plan on," I mused. "But we could've done a hell of a lot worse." And it wasn't as if we wouldn't take a trip when the time was right. The sudden decision to fly to Vegas and elope meant bypassing all the usual milestones, including the honeymoon

It also meant keeping things quiet for the time being. The last thing we wanted was to take any attention from the happy couple, who now sat locked together and sipping champagne.

"There you are!" Magnus called out loud enough for all heads to turn our way. "Took you long enough."

"Whiskey dick, maybe..." Ari high-fived Magnus, laughing.

"I don't know what you're talking about." Pepper was prim and withdrawn once we reached the group. "All I wanted was to take a walk. You guys need to get your minds out of the gutter."

That was what got everybody laughing harder than ever, though when I glanced Barrett's way, I noticed his laughter died way sooner than everyone else's.

5

CONNOR

"The last time you were on a yacht before a wedding, you were wearing a blinking dick on your head." I had to grin as I reminded Pepper of the antics revolving around Lourde's bachelorette party. "I wouldn't blame you if you can't remember. You were pretty wasted that night."

Pepper made a point of meeting my gaze in the mirror, where she took one last look at her sexy, summery dress so I could witness the way she rolled her eyes. "I wasn't that wasted. I remember everything."

"You were cute as hell that night." Approaching her from behind, I wrapped my arms around her slim waist and had the pleasure of admiring her reflection. "Come to think of it, you're cute as hell every day."

She turned to me, smirking a little as she wound her arms around my waist. "You don't need to lay it on so thick," she purred. "If I didn't know better, I would think you were feeling guilty or something. Kissing a little ass to throw me off track."

"But you do know better," I reminded her, kissing the tip

of her nose while shamelessly groping her. It was our honeymoon, after all, even if we were the only ones who knew about it. "I don't know. I guess it's something about being here and witnessing another milestone. Knowing we had a milestone of our own. It's got me thinking, I guess."

"Good things?" She pulled her head back a little before her eyebrows knitted together. There was loving concern in her voice when she asked, "Is everything all right?"

"Oh, yeah. Everything's great. Nothing to worry about." When her penetrating stare remained focused on me, I chuckled. "I shouldn't have said anything. I don't need you thinking I'm... I don't know, second-guessing things."

"I know you aren't," she retorted like the little smartass she was. "Because you would be a fucking idiot if you were second-guessing us."

With a growl, I pulled her closer, running my hand over her ass before slapping it. "Careful, or we'll miss boarding the yacht. I'll be too busy punishing you."

"Ooh, I'm shivering." She even gave me a dramatic shudder and managed not to crack a smile until I did. "Was that convincing?" she whispered.

"Let's just say you'd better not try to make it as an actress." I checked the time on my phone and winced at how late it already was. "Come on. We better move. I don't need one of those wedding planners getting on my ass for throwing the schedule off."

Something almost wistful passed over Pepper's face. She probably thought I didn't notice, but I noticed everything about her. "You know..." I offered as we left our rooms and headed down the east wing hall, "... we can do it right if you want to. We can have the whole party, the guests, every-thing. Nobody ever has to know we got married already."

"Oh, I know. I'm not worried about that." There was

something strained in her voice that told me otherwise. "Besides, it's your wedding too. And I totally respect that you didn't want to go all out and make a big deal about it. People do that all the time, and for what? To show off?" She winced, looking around with her teeth bared in a grimace. "I probably shouldn't say that so loud around here," she added before wincing again.

The controlled chaos had broken out shortly after dawn, which was unfortunate, considering we hadn't finished our third round of sex until a couple of hours before that. I tried and failed to stifle a yawn, thanks to the dozens of workers buzzing around the place.

As we reached the top of the stairs, I turned to her and took her hands in mine. "We can still have a party," I told her and meant it. "We know we are completely committed to each other, which is what matters. There's nothing wrong with showing off if that's what you really want."

She didn't deserve to suffer for the bullshit my parents went through. If I'd spent years not seeing the point of committed relationships, it was largely thanks to witnessing the two of them. Everything was for show to keep up appearances and our social standing. By the time Ari and Olivia's wedding had rolled around, they were essentially divorced in every meaningful sense of the word. There was nothing between them anymore, barely a semblance of a true relationship. I wanted no part of that charade. I wanted us to be authentic and even spontaneous, which was why a trip to Vegas seemed like a no-brainer.

"Uncle Connor!" The sound of feet slapping the hardwood floor followed my nephew's joyful cry. As always, Colton was a tornado on two legs, running full speed toward me with his arms outstretched.

I caught him and swung him around, laughing at the

way he giggled. "What are you doing?" I asked after hugging him. "Where's Naomi?"

"There you are!" The girl looked beyond frazzled as she jogged down the hall. "I'm sorry, Mr. Diamond."

"You don't have to apologize. I know how slippery this one can be," I added, tickling Colton's stomach until he shouted with laughter.

"I come with you!" he announced. As usual, he was very determined.

"I'm sorry, big guy. Not this time." The kid knew how to pull off a killer pout that could take an uncle's heart and crush it into pulp. "But hey, it's not like you're here alone. Right? You have Noah here. You guys can play all day, so long as you get lots of rest before tomorrow. It's going to be a big day."

"I'll take him back to Noah's room," Naomi offered, and I set him back on the floor before she took his hand to lead him away. I caught the same wistful look on Pepper's face she was wearing earlier when we talked about the wedding. The time would come for us, I had no doubt. Watching my friends start their families was enough to get me thinking in that direction too. They'd shown me it was possible to be involved parents and have a life at the same time. Kids didn't mean the end of anything.

We started down the stairs, and the girl who'd first greeted us on arrival released a heavy sigh when she spotted us. "Great, you're here. Everyone else is already out on the dock. There's plenty of food on the yacht." She must have been a shepherd in a former life since she had no problem herding us out the door and down to the docks that were part of the estate's eastern border. I spotted everyone waiting down there, and it was my sister who first noticed us, waving an arm over her head.

When Barrett noticed, he followed the direction her attention had taken. Even at a distance, it was clear his smile turned to something else. I noticed it at the bonfire after Pepper and I returned from our trip to the boathouse.

It didn't completely disappear by the time we reached the group, either. I hadn't mentioned it to Pepper, figuring I could be imagining things. I didn't want to start trouble during the wedding. That was why we kept our wedding a secret, anyway. Nothing worse than someone who pulled focus from the bride and groom.

Besides, it seemed like Ari's head would explode if anything went wrong.

"She's determined to make it," he was telling Olivia once they began boarding the yacht. "I keep telling her if your health won't allow it..." He could've only been referring to his grandmother, who hadn't been in great health but was as stubborn as her grandson. Nothing would stop her if she was determined to make it to the wedding.

Olivia was his calming influence, touching his chest once they were on deck. "Hey. She didn't live as long as she has by making stupid decisions, right? We have to trust your grandmother knows what she's talking about. If she feels well enough to be here, she will be, and she wouldn't want you worrying about her. So don't make me tell on you for worrying yourself sick because you know I will, and Grandma Farrah listens to me." There was a twinkle in her eye when she said it, but I had no doubt she meant it.

As the yacht set off, we sat down at a table so full of food I was amazed it didn't crack under the weight. Every kind of fruit and pastry known to man was already set out, along with an elaborate charcuterie board that took up half the table. Beside us stood a chef ready to prepare fresh crêpes and omelets.

"How are you guys?" Lourde asked, waving a hand when one of the stewards offered a mimosa. "No, thank you. I'll just stick to tea this morning."

"I should be the one asking you how you are," I observed with a sympathetic frown before accepting a Bloody Mary. "You feeling all right? Too much sangria last night, sis?"

"My stomach is just a little funny. No biggie." However, she snagged a chocolate croissant from one of the serving trays on the table before taking her next breath. I guessed chocolate didn't count as something worth avoiding when she had an upset stomach.

In an effort to engage Barrett, I said, "I don't know how that kid of yours isn't the most spoiled brat in the whole world. It's impossible to say no to him without wanting to offer like a million bucks to make up for it."

He snorted, but it was half-hearted. "Tell me about it. When he puts on that pout, he might as well punch me in the face."

"It's only going to get worse as they get older," Olivia predicted. "They're going to be a handful."

"With their genes?" Evelyn pointed out, and the girls giggled with her. "It's inevitable."

"So this is what we've become." Magnus looked around the table and tried to seem disappointed, fighting back a grin. "A few years ago, we were running Manhattan, keeping entire bars and clubs in business thanks to all the money we spent there and the business we brought in just for being who we were. Now look at us. We're sitting around on a yacht, talking about our kids."

"And those of us who don't have kids have nothing to add to the conversation," Pepper pointed out with a wry smirk. There were no feelings behind it. She wasn't hurt. She made a good point, though. So did Magnus.

"That's how it goes," I summed up before lifting my glass. "To new beginnings. For the happy couple and all of us."

"I'll drink to that," Evelyn agreed with a sunny smile, kissing her husband on the cheek before raising her mimosa.

Once we had finished our toast, Barrett's gaze weighed on me again. "New beginnings? What's new with you guys?" he asked, but an undercurrent of bitterness ran through the question, though I didn't have the first clue where it came from.

"Yes." Lourde practically pounced on us, leaning in. All it took was Barrett easing the door open a crack for her to barrel through. "When is it going to be your turn? I mean, no offense or anything, but you've been together forever. I'm looking forward to watching my brother tie the knot."

Of all times for Pepper to sit back mutely and let me stumble my way through an answer, the fact that all eyes were now on us was no help. "Oh, you know," I replied, deliberately vague. "When the time is right. It's not like we never talk about it."

"That's reassuring." Lourde rolled her eyes at me, scoffing. "And romantic too."

"I thought we were supposed to be talking about them?" I waved an arm toward Ari and Olivia, though they seemed amused at where the conversation had gone.

"It's okay," Ari offered, chuckling. "We don't mind having to share the spotlight for a minute, and it's a good question."

Of course, they would decide to bust my balls about this.

It was a good thing the steward announced that the chef was ready to begin preparing our meals, distracting the group from their interrogation. Lourde murmured something to Barrett, who shook his head with a scowl before exchanging a look with Magnus I couldn't make sense of. *What the hell was going on?*

I'd had enough by the time Barrett joined me in front of the omelet station, where I looked over the filling options. "Hey, can I ask you something?" I ventured, hoping I wouldn't regret it. I'd known him long enough to know this wasn't something that would go away on its own. When he started brooding, he could make it an Olympic sport. Normally, though, he didn't conceal his thoughts for long.

"Sure. What's up?" There was tension in his voice and his stony expression. He wouldn't look me in the eye. Like I was talking to a stranger rather than my lifelong friend and brother-in-law.

"Well, that's what I want to ask you." With one eye on the rest of the group, I muttered, "Are you pissed at me?"

He scoffed, still avoiding eye contact. "Why would I be pissed at you?"

"That's what I would like to know. Why *would* you be?" I insisted. Nothing was more frustrating than talking to a brick wall, which was what this felt like. "It seems we need to clear the air since we'll be hanging around here for a few days. I don't want this weird vibe between us."

He was fighting with himself. That much was obvious, his jaw ticking, nostrils flaring before he released a sigh. "There's something we should talk about when we get back to the house," he settled for grunting, keeping his voice low. "I'm going out of my way to keep things quiet for Pepper's sake, and I would suggest you do the same."

"What the hell does that mean?" I asked, stunned. We may as well have been engaged in two different conversations for all the sense he was making.

Before he could reply, Pepper joined us. "Do you have a second?" she murmured, looking pained. I noticed her phone clutched in her hand. "I think we have a little problem."

I had to pretend I didn't hear how Barrett snorted behind me.

What did he think he knew?

And why did he seem so pissed at me about it?

6

CONNOR

"They're going live with the photos tomorrow." Pepper paced the study below deck, occasionally running her fingers over the spines of leatherbound books lined up in neat rows along mahogany bookshelves. "So there goes our secret. I think it would be better if we came out and told everybody." I couldn't tell whether she was more disappointed or angry at having our hand forced by the paparazzi. Knowing her the way I did, the latter was more likely.

It went to show that no matter how well a person tried to prepare, there was no covering every base. My head fell back before I let out a groan. "We were so fucking careful. How did somebody get our pictures?"

"I don't know, but they did," she muttered darkly. As I watched, she pulled a book from a shelf and looked for a second like she wanted to throw it before changing her mind and sliding it into place again. "So much for not wanting to steal their thunder."

"It'll be much worse if we wait for the pictures to go public and everybody finds out that way," I pointed out.

"Nobody has to kiss our asses. We'll announce our wedding, and that will be it."

No, it wasn't the way we wanted to break the news, but the world had a way of forcing our hands sometimes. "It is what it is," I offered, kissing the top of Pepper's head when she paced her way to me and came to a stop. "And it's one more thing to celebrate. This doesn't have to be a bad thing."

"Okay." She took a deep breath that she let out all at once before her full lips pulled into a smirk. "Let's go explain to our friends and family why we eloped and didn't invite anybody. I'm sure this is going to go really well."

"I love your positive attitude." I loved everything about her. I loved how concerned she was over what her friends would think and not in a status symbol way as my mother would. She didn't want to hurt anybody's feelings. I honestly couldn't remember a time when my mother ever operated that way.

There was something in the air when we returned to the group. It had nothing to do with the breeze coming off the water or the omelets being cooked up. A sense of foreboding washed over me when I met a half-dozen wary gazes. "What did we miss?" I asked, looking around.

"You weren't supposed to say anything," Lourde told Barrett in a tight whisper that wasn't anywhere near soft enough for me not to hear. "Remember?"

His scowl deepened before he grunted, "I'm sorry, but seeing as how we might have to pay a lot of money to stop the story from going public, I can't sit back and pretend everything's fine. Maybe we should ask your brother for the truth."

It was like I was living in a surreal nightmare as Barrett sat back, folding his arms and looking me up and down. "Are you sure you haven't done any traveling lately?" he asked while the rest of the group remained silent but watchful.

Pepper squeezed my hand. "What is this really about?" she asked with an edge to her voice. "It's like we're in front of a firing squad."

"None of this is your fault," Barrett told her, but it was almost like an afterthought before he glared at me again. "I'm sorry, really. I'm sorry for bringing it up like this, but I can't sit here and pretend everything's fine. Connor, have you been to Vegas lately?"

Pepper and I exchanged a glance. "How did you know about that?" I asked.

"Did you know, Pepper?" Lourde asked in a soft voice. I couldn't tell what she hoped the answer would be, but she sounded as if she was ready to cry. Like something terrible had happened. It was bizarre.

"I mean... yes?" Pepper blurted out a laugh that seemed to take everyone by surprise. "What are you getting at? Out with it already. I want to eat."

Barrett heaved a sigh. "Fine, then. We'll do it your way. Lourde got a call yesterday from a friend who works for *TMZ*. Connor, they got a hold of some pictures of you in Vegas. They're planning on publishing them soon. He didn't have any specifics, but he used the word partying, and I think we all know what that means..." He paused like he wanted to let the words sink in. "It sounded like it was pretty wild. It's probably better that you have the heads-up, anyway, so you're not blindsided by this."

"Barrett was going to reach out to see if he could kill the story," Lourde explained. I could almost taste her disappointment. "But honestly, I think you should be the one to do it. This is your mess."

"All we ask is that you try to keep it quiet." Ari was stern, lowering his brow like a bull ready to charge. "The timing is shit, but it is what it is."

"We just want everything to be all right with you guys," Olivia insisted. "Whatever you guys need, we're here for you."

I couldn't come up with anything to say. When I looked at Pepper again, it was obvious she was as dumbfounded as I was. "I don't understand what's going on," she admitted with a soft laugh. "You think Connor was partying in Vegas without me and the paparazzi took pictures?"

"That's what happened." Barrett scowled at me while Lourde looked completely distraught for Pepper. "Nobody wanted you to find out this way."

Part of me knew it wouldn't be received well if I laughed. But dammit, the whole thing was so ridiculous, I couldn't help it. "Oh, fuck me. And here we are, trying to avoid causing trouble." I pulled Pepper in close to my chest, and she burst out laughing like I did, winding her arms around my waist.

"Connor wasn't partying... not by himself," she told them between fits of giggles. "I was with him!"

"You... were there? But he didn't say..." Lourde looked at Barrett and put a hand over her mouth as her eyes went wide.

"And we didn't go out there to party," I explained. It was sort of fun watching Barrett realize he jumped to the wrong conclusion. "We didn't want to tell anybody because we didn't want to steal focus from Ari and Olivia."

Olivia got it first. Her mouth fell open before she gasped and pointed at us. "Did you get married?" she squealed.

"Oh my God!" Lourde jumped out of her chair. "Are you serious? You eloped?"

"Surprise?" Pepper squeaked out before shrugging. "We

didn't want to wait anymore. It's not that we didn't want you guys there. We just didn't want to steal any attention. But it looks like we did, anyway," she concluded and sighed.

"We had no idea it would blow up like this. And in case you're wondering..." I added, turning to Barrett, "... we were about to announce it when we came back up here because Pepper heard about the photos. We figured we should break the news before somebody did it for us."

It was no surprise when the girls immediately jumped on Pepper, hugging and giving her shit at the same time for keeping it a secret. "Mom and Dad are never going to get over this!" Lourde groaned, not that their opinion mattered much to me.

"Congrats, man. It's about time." Magnus shook my hand before clapping me on the back. "There I was, figuring you'd be the last to get married."

"It was one of those impulsive things," I explained with a shrug before shaking Ari's outstretched hand.

"Sorry to give you shit like that," he said, shaking his head. "It sounded like you were out there, fucking around on Pepper. We all jumped to conclusions, I guess."

Right, thanks to somebody who steered them in that direction.

Barrett cleared his throat and ran a hand over the back of his neck. I'd seen him look shamefaced before, but this had to be a new record. Rather than let him off the hook right away, I let him dangle for a bit, waiting for him to make the first move. I didn't want to make it too easy. Sure, he'd offered to pay to kill the story, but he could have come straight to me with it rather than bring it up in front of the whole group.

"Listen," he began in a gruff tone. "I was wrong. I should've gone to you with this right away. I didn't know how to properly navigate it. I was trying to avoid a scandal during the wedding, but I was also pissed at you because it looked like you fucked up a good thing."

When I considered it from his point of view, I had to appreciate how much he cared. "I get it."

"So we good then?" he asked. The concern in his voice almost made up for the disdain I'd heard earlier when he sat in judgment of me with only half the facts in his pocket.

I could only scoff at us being anything less than okay. "This is a drop in the bucket compared to some of the shit you've pulled. And it's not like I've never pulled off shit of my own," I added with a smirk. That was putting it mildly. If anything, his knowledge of my checkered past made it easier for him to believe I would do something like what he had assumed.

"You idiot." Lourde gave me a gentle punch on my arm before wrapping her arms around me and resting her head on my shoulder. "I can't believe I missed watching you get married. I was really hoping I could get to see that. It's such a big, monumental event." Her voice got thicker with every word until it sounded like she was on the verge of tears.

"Hell, I didn't know it would affect you that much," I offered in lieu of an apology. When it seemed like that didn't do anything to ease her feelings, I hugged her. "You know how I feel about the big, flashy shit," I murmured low enough for only her to hear. "I didn't want some overblown event like Mom and Dad had. I figured maybe if we started things off differently, we could end them differently."

Her eyes shone with understanding when she looked up at me, and we shared the kind of smile only siblings can share. People who came from the same parents and household understood things on a deeper level without having to say a word. "I get it. But I could tell you there's no chance of you and Pepper ending up like they have. They didn't marry for love. You did. Right off the bat, it's a much better start."

"I know you're right." All at once, her eyes filled with tears, and I rubbed her back. "Are you okay? You seem a little off." Maybe more like an emotional basket case, but experience told me women didn't like hearing that kind of thing, even from their brothers. Maybe especially from their brothers.

She waved a hand before running that hand under her leaking eyes. "I'm always overly emotional about weddings, and now there's two for me to cry over." At least she was laughing, even if it was shaky.

"See? That's why it's a good thing we eloped," I joked. "We spared you the dehydration from your crying eyes out during the ceremony." Her withering glare told me she wouldn't start sobbing, which was the point. "Now, I need you to do something for me," I added.

"What?" she asked.

"I need you to help me take everybody's mind off this and put the attention back on the people we're here for. Can you do that?"

Her jaw tightened with resolve before her head bobbed up and down. "Can I do that?" She blew out a breath before spinning on her heel and flapping her arms around, gaining attention.

"Okay, everybody! Back to brunch, and then I plan to lay out for a little while. I need some color if I don't want to look like a ghost in all those wedding photos."

"Don't get burned!" Olivia warned. "Sunburned skin doesn't go with a peach dress, and Pepper told me about the time you fell asleep and burned lobster red under the Hamptons sun a few years ago!"

Pepper flashed me a grin from across the deck, and I

returned it. It felt better, really, now that everybody knew. There were no secrets to be kept and no reason for Barrett to stare daggers at me anymore.

"You know," I murmured, turning to Ari. "I could still have the story killed. Really, I would rather make the announcement about our marriage than have it come out in *TMZ*. If you think it will pull focus from you guys on your big day, consider it done." And it would mean avoiding a blow-up with my parents once word reached them.

"Fuck that," he immediately replied. "I can accept that you eloped and escaped all this planning and bullshit. You don't get to avoid a media blow-up too. That's not fair."

"Misery loves company?" Magnus suggested, grinning as he lifted a Bloody Mary to his lips.

"I heard that," Olivia called out. When he looked her way, she narrowed her eyes at him. "Let's not even use the word misery today." He responded with a salute before we settled back in to enjoy the day as planned.

7

ARI

Would they show up in pictures if I slipped a bottle of Pepto-Bismol into each of my front pockets? What if I tucked them in my suit jacket later?

Maybe Connor and Pepper did things the right way. Perhaps I should have suggested to Olivia that we elope. It would have meant avoiding a shit ton of last-minute plan changes, conflicts with the vendors, and miscommunications.

"You okay there, buddy?" It was Barrett's idea that we spend a couple of hours fishing the morning of the wedding. It was an excuse to get away from the estate for a little while and clear my head when there had been nothing but to-do lists running through it for weeks. I thought the bride was supposed to be the one handling all that shit, but it turned out that even with the help of the bride and a pair of highly respected planners, there were still endless questions to be answered and plans to be approved.

"You're not getting cold feet, are you?" Connor was

enjoying himself way more than he should, leaning back in his chair with his fishing pole in one hand.

None of us had gotten so much as a nibble in the hour since we'd come out, but catching a big one wasn't the point. And I got the feeling that if I came home covered in fish stench, Olivia's head would explode. If not hers, then one of the planners.

"About Olivia? Fuck no." I didn't have to think about it, not about her. Sure, it wasn't love at first sight, but that didn't mean it wasn't just as real. If anything, what we had was stronger. We had started out at each other's throats and ended up ready to build a life together. That meant overcoming all the shit that had tried to keep us apart and building a strong foundation from which everything else would grow.

"You're not doing your own vows or anything, are you?" Magnus reeled in his line a bit before cracking open a beer. "That's one thing I regret. Having to come up with my vows."

"You didn't do too bad," I offered, thinking back. "I mean, it was short, but you got the point across."

"Oh, there's a ringing endorsement," Barrett muttered, snorting. "Short, sweet, got the point across."

Once he finished laughing, Magnus shrugged. "You know, I don't remember a damn thing about it. And I don't mean because some time has passed. By the end of the ceremony, I couldn't remember a word I said. I was in a trance or some shit."

"That's something Lourde told me after our reception," Barrett mused, staring out over the water. I couldn't read his face, thanks to his sunglasses, but he sounded thoughtful. "As soon as it was over, she wondered where the day went. Everything goes by so fast."

I could only snicker to myself because I wished I had

that problem. I wanted it to be over if only to be on the other side of my anxiety. "I want it to be perfect for her," I confess. "I know it sounds corny and pathetic, but that's why I'm all full of nerves today. When she looks back on this in fifteen or twenty years, I don't want there to be a single thing she regrets or wishes we had done differently."

For a while, the only sound came from water lapping against the sides of the boat and seagulls in the distance. It would've been a perfectly peaceful, beautiful day except for ominous clouds rolling in from the west—yet another point of concern. I had been checking the weather apps for two weeks, tracking today's outlook. "Those clouds don't look good," I muttered, and the pit in my stomach grew.

"It's been cloudy and shitty-looking on and off for days," Connor reminded me. "And it always clears up. You'll be fine."

"You want to know what I think?" Barrett asked, tossing an empty beer can into the cooler. "I think if Olivia is still dwelling on your wedding twenty years from now, she's not who I thought she was. I mean, there would be twenty years of memories between now and then, right? You have a son together. You have your careers. She won't be obsessing over a little detail of a big day twenty years from now. She'll be thinking back on her marriage and her family. Her life."

It was Connor who broke the silence. "Don't tell me that's what you plan on using for your best man's speech later."

Barrett groaned. "Fuck off." There would be no chance of catching anything with the four of us laughing as hard as we did and scaring off every fish in a hundred-yard radius, but it didn't matter.

Though even as I laughed, I couldn't get the thought of

those clouds out of my head. It didn't help that they kept coming closer every minute.

"They say rain is good luck on a wedding day." Those were the first words my grandmama offered on arriving at the mansion after being escorted up the front stairs by one of the butlers hired for the day's events.

Guests had started arriving a half hour earlier and, from the sound of it, were enjoying cocktails and hors d'oeuvres on the back terrace and the lawn leading down to the ceremony area. A stiff breeze stirred the flowers on the front patio and tore a few rose petals free to twist in the wind before blowing away.

"I'm still hoping it passes with nothing." However, every hour that passed told me it was less and less likely. The day had gone from clear and sunny to gray, but as of thirty minutes before the ceremony, that gray was beginning to turn to a deeper shade of charcoal while thunder rumbled in the distance.

Grandmama grimaced, taking my arm and allowing me to walk her into the house. "Trust me. Once you reach my age, your joints become a better forecaster than anybody you'll see on the Weather Channel."

I could hear the discomfort in her voice, and it concerned me. "I'm just glad you could make it. Are you sure you're up to—"

She cut me off with an impervious glare, arching an eyebrow. "I can manage myself, thank you. I wouldn't miss today for anything in the world." She patted my cheek, smiling fondly now that her glare had softened. She had a way of swinging from one extreme to the other at times. "My grandson, taking this big step. Then again, you do already have a child together..."

She could pretend all she wanted to be faintly scandalized at Noah being born out of wedlock, but it was a different story when he came running our way through the entry hall. My heart jumped into my throat when he came dangerously close to crashing into a vase full of roses and hydrangeas, but he managed to sidestep it at the last second. "There's my handsome little man," she exclaimed, and I bent to pick him up so she could kiss his cheek.

"You'd better be careful," I warned him, smoothing down his hair and straightening his bowtie. "You don't want to ruin your suit before the wedding. You have to look nice when you bring the rings down the aisle for me and Mommy. Can you do that?"

"Can I have a cookie?" Because for a two-year-old, things really were that simple.

"I'll make a deal with you." Grandmama winked at me, taking Noah's hand once I set him on his feet. "We'll find you a cookie, but you have to sit down like a good little boy and eat it rather than running around with it and getting it all over yourself. Deal?"

He nodded happily, and she led him outside to where a sweets table had been set up along with the other hors d'oeuvres. At this rate, I had to wonder if everything would be safe out there. We had an awning to protect the food from rain, but the wind was getting a little stronger every minute. I was starting to wonder if we shouldn't rush the ceremony if only to get it over with before all hell broke loose.

The photographer found me pacing the entry hall like the worried groom I was. "We'd like to get some shots of you and the groomsmen," she said, waving me outside while an assistant followed on her heels.

I could understand now why Lourde had said their big day had passed in a blur. That was how it felt to be pushed and pulled from one place to another. It seemed like I had been running nonstop since our return from the boat—we had already captured the groomsmen's preparations, gotten photos with Noah, and I had gifted the guys the monogrammed flasks I'd commissioned for them. How was it the ceremony was so close already?

"How's that stomach treating you?" Barrett asked when I reached the front lawn, where he and the rest of the guys were assembled to greet guests as they arrived.

"I pretty much chugged something to settle it," I admitted while smiling and waving to people who looked vaguely familiar. Friends of my grandmama's, I assumed. "This storm isn't helping it."

For the first time, he looked concerned as he scanned the sky. "Yeah, it's not looking so great. Let's hope it holds off until after the ceremony, then everyone can go to the tents." They were sturdy enough, for sure, and large enough to fit two hundred guests for dinner and dancing. From where we stood, I could see staff members rushing around in there, putting the final touches on the décor and the place settings. "I hope like hell the clouds clear up in time for the fireworks."

"And everything is in place for my surprise?" I asked Barrett, whose sole job that day was to track Reilly Kissinger's arrival and handle any problems that might arise.

"Everything is on track," he assured me. "The helicopter arrives at nine o'clock on the dot, even if the skies do open," he continued. "Anything that blows through should be out to sea by then. I have Connor checking the weather reports too. We've got you covered."

"All right, guys. Let's get together here." The photographer waved her hands, motioning for us to stand closer at the base of the stairs with the mansion behind us.

"Remember when we used to go to weddings and see who could be the first to screw a bridesmaid?" Magnus muttered through a smile as the photos were snapped. "Those were the days."

"No," I grunted, smiling for the camera. Not that I thought he truly meant it. It was more of a joke meant to ease my tension, but I felt it needed to be said. When I looked back at that version of myself and how empty his life was, I hardly recognized him. "These are the days."

We finished, and Magnus handed me my flask, which I noticed was no longer empty when I took it from him. "Here's my contribution to your mental well-being," he told me with a grin, touching his flask to mine before we both took a swig.

"Shaking off those last-minute jitters?" I turned at the question, vaguely recognizing the voice. Once I identified my father standing at my mother's side, it was no surprise that the voice was only faintly recognizable to my ears. I was more surprised they'd managed to fly in from their estate in Florence for the ceremony. As it was, they had cut it pretty close.

"Everything looks beautiful." My mother air kissed both of my cheeks before taking my hands. She was perfectly groomed, as always. Flawless. And for once, she looked genuinely happy. "You've done a wonderful job planning this, and I'm sure Olivia will be a beautiful bride."

"Here's hoping you get through the ceremony before the clouds open," my father joked, staring at the sky. "Even a

Farrah Goldsmith original won't hold up against a torrential downpour."

"Why don't I show you over to the ceremony area?" Barrett greeted them warmly before escorting them away before I could burst a blood vessel. Though I didn't hold anything against them, and there were no hard feelings, my grandmama had been more of a parent to me than either of them could ever have hoped to be. If they hadn't made it, I would've gotten over it without trying. If she had missed this, I imagined I would have felt strangely empty.

Magnus gave me a gentle shove from behind before passing me. "We should all get over there," he pointed out, and now I noticed the wedding planners and various staff herding the guests out to the rows of white chairs arranged in front of the floral arch. Beyond it, waves crashed dramatically as the storm built.

Mother Nature had decided to RSVP.

What a shame she couldn't have been late to the event.

8

ARI

This was it.

All the planning had led to this moment, where I waited beneath an arch dripping with fragrant blooms. I had my best friends at my back. The love of my life was about to emerge from the house and make the dramatic walk down the back stairs on her father's arm. They would travel down a snow-white runner lined on both sides by potted, flowering trees that ran from the far end of the runner up to the front row of chairs. My parents sat with Grandmama on one side while Olivia's mom sat across from them.

We shared a smile, and her chin quivered with emotion.

The faint strains of "Canon in D" floated through the air as the string quartet began to play. I stiffened my spine while my pulse raced, and the wedding procession began. Evelyn went first, holding Noah's hand and helping him down the stairs. Once they reached the lawn, she crouched down a bit and pointed to me, murmuring instructions. I couldn't pretend my heart wasn't in my throat as he began his walk, holding the satin pillow containing our rings. It seemed if anything, he enjoyed the attention, beaming as guests chuckled and sighed over his navy blue suit, a miniature version of the suits the guys and I wore.

"Daddy!" It was like he finally noticed I was waiting for him once he was halfway down the aisle, and from that point, he ran full-out, carrying the pillow by one corner. There was a reason the rings were held in place with a length of ribbon tied in a bow.

"Thank you, pal." I gave him a fist bump and ruffled his hair before Grandmama reached for him, motioning for him to join her. As soon as he was settled, it was Evelyn's turn, followed by Pepper, and finally, Lourde as Matron of Honor. The girls wore matching originals—floor length, strapless sheath dresses featuring a length of sheer crêpe sewn in at the waist and gathered to cover one shoulder. The light peach color, one of the year's most popular, complemented our navy suits and was also featured in their bouquets and the archway over my head.

"We did well for ourselves, didn't we?" Barrett murmured with his eyes glued to his wife as she finished the procession.

I couldn't respond. The girls were assembled, and the guests rose, all of us looking toward the house in anticipation. This was it. Everything had led to this. All the waiting, even when I didn't know I was waiting. How could I have imagined there was a woman out there so completely perfect for me?

I could barely breathe as she came into view on her father's arm, and a gasp of admiration rose over the guests as Olivia and her father began to descend. The dramatic lace train and Olivia's antique lace veil trailed behind them.

It didn't surprise me when she'd announced she wanted something timeless and classic. She was not a woman who bowed to trends. With that in mind, the team designed a silk gown with a mermaid skirt entirely overlaid with the finest antique lace from Burano, Italy, for her. It featured a sweetheart neckline with loosely draped sleeves that barely touched her elbows. In front of her was an enormous peach and cream bouquet, and last I'd heard, my grandmama had given Olivia a lace handkerchief to tie around the stems as her 'something borrowed.'

More than anything, it was her smile that held my attention. She was radiant, glowing, a princess floating down the aisle surrounded by adoring guests. This was what she deserved, nothing less, and joy shone from her tear-filled eyes when they met mine.

I had to remind myself to breathe as she came closer.

Once they reached us, Olivia's father shook my hand. "You know we wish you nothing but the best," he murmured. "You take care of her now."

"That's all I ever want to do," I assured him before he turned to Olivia and kissed her cheek. They exchanged a few quiet words before she handed her bouquet to Lourde, then took my hand.

It was electric, the touch of her skin. Everything slid into place and the world went silent and still for one brief moment.

Everything made sense.

That was until a gust of wind stirred her veil, along with nervous laughter from the guests. "Maybe we should make this quick?" she whispered, comically grimacing before we turned to the officiant.

"In case I forget to tell you..." I whispered, "... you're the most beautiful bride who ever lived, and I'm the luckiest man on Earth." I left out the part where I couldn't wait to peel that dress off and ravish her since it didn't seem the most appropriate time.

The thought was there. But then it usually was.

"We gather today to celebrate this beautiful couple." The officiant was an old friend of Olivia's parents, and he smiled fondly at her. "It's a great honor and privilege to watch as two lives are united, but especially when there is already so much love between them..."

There was no keeping my thoughts from wandering as he went on. I couldn't think about anything but Olivia's grace and beauty and how fucking lucky I was to be the man standing at her side. I promised myself then and there that I would do everything in my power for the rest of my life to live up to the standard she deserved. I would be the man she needed me to be. I would make sure she never for a minute regretted joining her life with mine.

We turned to each other at the officiant's request, taking each other's hands. Hers were trembling, but when I looked up from them into her shining eyes, nothing but love and excitement were there. I took a handkerchief from my breast pocket and dabbed a tear away from her cheek, cueing laughter from the guests.

"Thanks," Olivia whispered, grinning through her tears.

"That's what I'm here for," I reminded her with a wink before reciting our vows.

The most profound sense of gratitude filled me as Olivia began the customary words. I had heard them before at countless weddings, though I wasn't usually paying much attention. Now, the meaning behind the simple statements struck me to my core. To have and to hold through everything that came along, the good and the bad. There would be storms—it didn't matter how much a person had in their bank account. Certain life situations were universal and couldn't be avoided, no matter a person's net worth. We would be together through all of that and more. We would hold each other up when the other was too weak to stand on their own.

"*All the days of my life*," she concluded, breaking into a huge smile when she did—one that was punctuated by a strong rumbling. Thunder rolled overhead, and I heard Noah whimper fretfully in his chair. The other kids would be inside with their nannies, but he'd be outside with us until the end of the ceremony.

We turned to him, and Olivia held out a hand. "Come here, sweetheart," she murmured, and everyone laughed indulgently as our son flew to his mother's side. She took one of his hands, and I took the other before I began my vows. Really, it was better this way. The three of us together, a family. Why shouldn't he be with us as I pledged my life to his mother?

"*In sickness and in health... to love, honor, and cherish...*" Another low rumble sounded, louder this time and strong enough to shake the ground slightly. For the first time, concern flashed in Olivia's eyes while Noah whimpered. "*All the days of my life*," I concluded before looking up at the ominous clouds.

From the corner of my eye, I saw Barrett extend his hand. In his open palm sat our rings. "You better hurry up," he murmured before an even louder crack of thunder shook the ground.

I wasted no time sliding the platinum band over Olivia's finger. No amount of cloud cover could dull the way the diamonds sparkled. The weight of the band around my finger was welcome. I wondered about that since it seemed strange to wear a ring when I wasn't accustomed to it, but it felt like the most natural thing in the world.

The officiant didn't hesitate to wrap things up. "Then, by the power vested in me, I declare they are man and wife. Aristotle, you may kiss your bride."

Finally. The best part. Olivia's kiss was sweet, tender, and filled with all the love she had shown me over the years and the love she would show me from this day forward. I had never felt so right. It was as if I was exactly where I belonged, holding my son's hand and kissing the love of my life while hundreds of guests applauded.

And the first big, fat raindrops began to fall.

Most storms started slowly. That had always been my experience, anyway. A little drizzle preceded the main event.

Not this time. We went from zero to downpour in about three seconds. A wall of water came down on us all at once, driven by wind and punctuated by thunderclaps. Somebody shouted, "Hurry! Inside!"

It was barely controlled chaos as guests began to flee across the lawn and up the steps into the house. I picked up Noah and immediately turned to my grandmama, who was being sheltered by a staff member holding an umbrella over her head. At some point during the ceremony, they had armed themselves and were now helping guests escape unscathed. I made a mental note to tip them more heavily than I had already planned.

Rather than let one of them shelter Olivia, I took the umbrella and held it over our heads while my parents helped Grandmama navigate the increasingly soaked ground. It was coming down hard enough that I could barely see where we were going, but we managed to make it down the aisle and up the stairs before Olivia dashed into the house with her arms crossed overhead. I could hear her laughter even over the thunder, the driving rain, and the shouts of confusion from the guests.

I set Noah down inside, and there was nothing to do but laugh. It didn't seem like anyone was in bad shape, and most everybody laughed it off along with me while looking outside. "That's one way to end a ceremony," I decided, laughing again.

I turned to my wife and kissed her again, and this time, our guests had the time to cheer us on. What a shame we had to keep things chaste in mixed company. There was something familiar in my wife's eyes once the kiss ended, and it told me she was thinking along the same lines.

"It looks like cocktail hour will take place indoors," one of the planners called out, already rearranging things while winding her way through the large group. "Once the storm passes, we can go to the tents."

I spotted Barrett standing nearby with Lourde and Colton. Waving him over, I asked, "Do you mind taking Noah to his nanny for me? Olivia will want to get changed into her reception dress."

"Isn't that something the bridesmaids could help with?" He was busting my balls, and I knew it. Smirking at him before taking Olivia by the waist, I turned her away from the French doors and the storm on the other side.

"Come on," I murmured in her ear. "Let's get you out of that wet dress."

9

ARI

It was a relief to escape to my suite at the far end of the west wing, which had doubled as the bridal suite today since it was the largest cluster of rooms in the mansion.

It was even nicer to close the door behind us and block out the roar two hundred guests created when they mingled in a ballroom.

"Do you think they got the food inside before the rain started?" Olivia removed her veil and laid it carefully across the back of an armchair. "We want to be sure everyone has enough to eat until the storm passes."

Her question went unanswered, thanks to the fact that I couldn't think of anything but how exquisite she looked. "You are the most stunning woman I've ever seen," I murmured, dumbstruck. "I don't know how I ended up with someone like you."

She turned away from the window, where she'd been checking out the storm's progress, and her smile made my heart skip a beat. "You're not so bad yourself. I've wanted to get my hands on you ever since I first saw you standing under that arch."

"I'm not doing much of anything else right now. Feel free to put your hands wherever you want." I sat on the edge of the bed, beckoning her. "Here. Let me unbutton you."

She turned her back to me, and I allowed my hands to trail over her bare skin before I started to work on the tiny buttons running from midway down her back to her tailbone. "My wife," I murmured, revealing more and more of her creamy skin with every button I undid.

"I like the sound of that." She sighed when I leaned in to brush my lips over her skin before undoing another button, then another.

"I like the sound of that too," I agreed. Spreading the dress open, I eased it down, letting it fall away from her body. "And I like the sight of this," I managed to choke out when her exquisite body sent all the blood in my brain rushing south.

She wore a pair of white lace panties and nothing else. With the silk and lace pooled around her, she slowly turned to face me. I had seen her body more times than I could count and touched, kissed, and worshiped every inch of it. Yet there was never a time she ceased to take my breath away.

She stepped out of the circle of material and into the circle of my arms, wrapping hers around my neck and leaning down until our mouths touched, allowing me to run my hands over her curves while my tongue stroked hers.

It took nothing to turn a spark into a flame, and soon, we were both rushing our way through undressing me. My skin burned where she made contact, the all-consuming fire that never failed to leap to life whenever we were together like this. No matter how many changes there were in our relationship or how being parents and business owners some-times put a strain on our schedules, we could always come back to this. The undeniable and unrelenting chemistry. The connection.

We were both laughing at our clumsy, frenzied fumbling by the time I stood and let my pants and boxer briefs slide to the floor. Turning her in place, I lowered her to the bed, peeling away her panties and tossing them aside before settling between her smooth, toned legs.

She draped one of them over my hip, drawing me closer, catching my mouth with hers and moaning into it when I wasted no time sinking into her familiar, welcome heat. I couldn't wait. Something urged me on, pushed me to take her.

As usual, she managed to sum it up in a handful of words. "Marriage is an aphrodisiac," she whispered before running her lips over my shoulder and biting down when I drove myself hard. Deep. She felt like fucking perfection.

She wasn't wrong. We had tied the knot and had the rings to prove it. That added something to the experience. Even though we had done this hundreds of times, I was making love to my wife now. Going slow, savoring every sigh, every whimper, savoring the taste of her skin and the sound of her helpless moans when I cupped one of her full tits and massaged it before pinching her nipple, rolling between my fingers the way she liked.

Her nails ran down my back, pressing just hard enough to leave me dancing on the line between pleasure and pain. I drove myself deeper, shaking the bed with every down-stroke, drawing soft grunts from her. "I love you," she breathed before moaning again when I rolled my hips, grinding my base against her clit.

"Fuck, I love you, Mrs. Goldsmith."

"Oh God, yes… don't stop…"

This was it.

All I'd ever want.

All I would ever need.

Her beautiful body, her skin against mine, her hips grinding into mine, increasing the friction, we lost ourselves to unspeakable pleasure that would only ever be shared by us—my wife and me.

"Are you going to come for me?" I murmured close to her ear when her cries rose in pitch, and her hips began to jerk frantically. "Are you going to come for your husband?"

"Fuck, yes!" She wrapped me in her arms and legs, clutching me close to her as her muscles closed around my cock in a vice grip so tight, I could barely move. "I'm going to come! Oh God, yes! Yes, Ari!"

Her back arched, and she gasped one last time before shuddering, giving herself over to the power of her orgasm while I worked for mine. Harder, faster, I let it consume me until there was nothing to do but let go and flood her with my seed. Somewhere in the back of my mind, I wondered if this would be the day we made another child together. It would be the bow on top of a perfect day.

For now, I settled for smiling down at her, taking in her flushed and dewy skin and dreamy expression once she opened her dark blue eyes. "There's no turning back now," I reminded her between gasps for air. "We consummated it."

"Good thing I had no intention of turning back." She kissed me once, then twice before I rolled away. She sat up and stretched before looking around the room. "We should probably get ourselves fixed up. There are still a lot of people down there who want a little time with us."

"You sound disappointed." I traced her spine with one finger until she shivered, giggling.

"Not disappointed. I would rather stay in here with you, that's all." She grinned at me over her shoulder. "But we have plenty of time for that, right? Two whole weeks."

After putting everything together, not to mention the usual stress of work, two weeks spent in Maui sounded like nothing short of paradise. "I can hardly wait to get you on the beach. You had better bring the skimpiest bikini you own." The idea made my dick twitch, which hardly seemed possible minutes after coming. Olivia tended to do that to me.

"Who needs a bikini?" She flashed an impish grin before barely escaping my greedy hands when I tried to grab her. "Don't get started now," she warned, jumping to her feet. "We really do need to get back downstairs."

Already, it sounded like the storm had begun to slow down. The pounding rain had softened, and any thunder was faint, distant.

Slowly, maybe even a little regretfully, I pieced myself back together before helping Olivia into her cream silk reception dress. Like the gown for the ceremony, it was simple but stunning. The bias-cut fabric hugged her curves, and its halter top displayed her perfectly sculpted shoulders. It was cut low in the back, almost down to her tailbone. "I can't guarantee I won't need a quickie later with you looking like this," I warned, letting my lips linger on her shoulder when she turned to check out her reflection in the full-length mirror.

"I can't guarantee I won't want one, with you looking hot as sin." Our eyes met in the mirror, and she chuckled. "Though really, this silk is not forgiving enough for that. I'd walk around all wrinkled, and everybody would know why."

"How about a quick blow job?" I countered. I wasn't

completely serious, which meant I could enjoy her throaty laughter.

"Is that what marriage means to you? Sex on demand?" She pouted her full lips after touching up her gloss and pretended to be insulted, but I knew better.

"Don't act like you're offended." Sliding my hands over her hips, I murmured, "Last I checked, you were just as much in a hurry to take my clothes off."

She lifted a shoulder. "Like I said, marriage is an aphrodisiac."

I would have my hands full with her, but I always knew that. It was a challenge I took on gladly. After she fixed her hair, which had gotten a little wet and then a little mussed from our activities, we stood face-to-face. I saw my entire world in her eyes. "Are you ready to head back down and party?" I asked, taking her hands and kissing them. The new diamond band was a nice addition. I looked forward to seeing it every day. "After everything it took to get us to this point, I think the least we're owed is a great party."

With that, we stepped out of the room, ready to start the rest of our lives together.

10

MAGNUS

"**I**s everything all right?" I asked Evelyn when she joined me after checking on Valentina and Aria. Once the worst of the wind and rain had passed, we were ushered to the main tent, and now guests mingled and chatted, waiting for the bride and groom to reappear.

"They're happy as clams," she confirmed. "Jess has them eating dinner with Colton, Noah, and the other nannies." If there was such a thing as angels, Jess was one of them. We could have never gotten by without her organization and energy.

"And how are you?" I asked before placing a lingering kiss on my wife's upturned mouth, only stopping when a telltale twitching in my pants told me I wouldn't be able to get away for much longer without an embarrassing public hard-on. There was something about her that made me lose control of myself.

She offered a secret, knowing grin once I let her up for air. "Better now," she purred, chuckling softly. "Something has you in a very good mood."

"I'm sure it has nothing to do with you looking like

living, breathing sex in that dress." I leaned down, nipping her earlobe with my teeth before whispering, "I can't wait to get you out of it later. What do you say we make an early exit?"

Her groan told me she was genuinely entertaining the idea but saw it wouldn't work. "You know how it is. If the bride or groom needs something..."

"I know." I didn't have to like it, but I knew. We had a job to do, even with countless staff members and two frantic wedding planners running around. We all had our jobs lined up tonight. My job was to make sure Ari's grandmother was taken care of, was feeling well, and to help her up to the room where she would spend the night if she were too tired.

After kissing my wife again, I decided to check on Farrah. As it turned out, I didn't need to. She was holding court with countless guests, telling stories of some of the clients she had dressed over the years. "I don't want to name names," she insisted, and somehow her voice rose over the giggles and questions coming from all directions. "I can't risk a lawsuit at my advanced age."

I managed to get close enough to lean down. "Can I get you anything?" I asked. "Something to eat? A drink?"

Although it wasn't technically time to begin dancing, the band had begun to play to keep the mood festive. I vaguely recognized the old song and the sound of it made her eyes light up. "How about a dance? It's been a long time since I've had the pleasure of cutting a rug with a handsome young man." I knew better than to refuse, and something told me she wouldn't care much that it wasn't time for dancing yet. When you were Farrah Goldsmith, you didn't need to rely on ceremony.

I led her across the floor laid especially for the event and stopped close to the bandstand, so we would stay out of the way of staff crisscrossing the space carrying trays of hors d'oeuvres and drinks. "Thank you," Farrah murmured once we were far away from the crowd. "You gave me the perfect getaway."

"You mean you don't really want to dance with me?" I frowned and stuck out my bottom lip. "I'm disappointed."

"You are too handsome and charming for your own good, but that's true of all you boys. And I suppose we ought to dance if only to keep up appearances." I was chuckling as I drew her closer, one hand at her waist while she closed her fingers around the other. We swayed slowly to the music while I made it a point to support her in case she felt weak. She put on a good show of being vital, but I knew what it was like to put on a show for the rest of the world.

Until I met Evelyn and figured out she was the only woman for me, I had done my share of pretending too.

"I have to say, it warms my heart to see all of you settling down with such wonderful girls." Her eyes might have faded with age, but they were still sharp when she looked up at me. "All of you did entirely too much running around. Naughty boys."

"We were young," I reminded her. "Nobody can say we didn't live."

"No, that much is true. Now it's time to settle down and build something real. I never doubted Aristotle had what it took to run the company, but he only started showing good sense when he recognized what a wonder Olivia is. I could finally rest easy when I knew he had found his partner... someone who would encourage him to be his very best. It seems like your Evelyn has done the same for you," she observed.

We looked across the room to where Evelyn sipped

champagne while chatting with Lourde. Whatever Lourde said made Evelyn throw her head back and laugh, and I couldn't help chuckling at the sight and sound. She was the textbook definition of someone who had come out of her shell, and I was so grateful she had. Not only for my sake, but for the rest of the world. She had so much talent, intelligence, and empathy to offer. Some people were hardened by their struggles, but Evelyn chose to use her experience to help others find the kind of fulfillment she'd found. It was a self-perpetuating loop since every person she helped left her more confident and determined to find others in need.

"We needed each other," I concluded. It was funny how easy it was to admit that to her. I wouldn't have been able to get the words out in front of my friends, and we had been through everything together. Maybe that was it. They knew me too well. Confessing to this kindly old woman was freeing in a way.

"It's a wonderful thing. Don't ever take it for granted." The song ended, and she patted my cheek with one gnarled hand, her skin paper thin—a reflection of time. "Thank you. That was delightful. Don't be surprised if I flag you down later the next time I'm cornered by gossip hounds."

I tucked her arm in the crook of my elbow before escorting her across the dance floor. "They were admirers," I countered. "They're dying to hear every word from your mouth."

"Again with the charm." She didn't have me fooled. The way her eyes twinkled told me she enjoyed a little charm now and then. "But I've spent too many years around people like that to see them as anything other than hungry little gossip hounds. I suppose I'm showing my age, becoming a curmudgeon."

"Don't sell yourself short." I kissed her cheek before

murmuring, "You are never too young to be curmudgeonly. Ask my wife. I can be pretty grumpy, myself." Farrah was laughing when I left her sitting with Ari's parents. His relationship with them was friendly enough, if not exactly warm or loving. The same seemed to be true of their relationship with Farrah, but I guessed it had something to do with the fact that they were never in town for very long, always jetting around the way they had been all of Ari's life.

That was one thing I would never do. My children would see me. They would know me. I had no interest in being an absentee parent.

That was one of many areas where Evelyn and I agreed. There were different reasons behind it. She had suffered for years under the cruelty and abuse of her monster of a father. There were still times when it amazed me that she and Barrett turned out as well as they had. Some people looked to their parents as an example of the kind of parent they wanted to be. She approached it from the opposite direction. She would be the parent he could never be. Our girls would never know what it meant to be openly mocked and ridiculed by a parent. They would only ever know love, support, and patience.

Lourde noticed something over my shoulders as I approached them, and the wide, knowing smile that spread across her face told me who I would find when I turned around. "It's about time!" she called out, teasing the happy couple as they entered the tent. Once the guests registered their presence, a round of applause rose along with the clinking of cutlery against champagne flutes. It only got louder when they kissed as requested, and the cameras flashing was almost blinding.

Once the commotion died down, they joined us and gladly accepted champagne from a passing server. "It is all so beautiful in here," Olivia sighed as she looked around the space. I couldn't pretend to disagree with the countless strings of lights strung up overhead, the over-the-top floral arrangements adorning every flat surface, and the candlelight. The effect was magic.

"You have a lot of very happy, impressed guests," I told her and Ari. "People are going to be talking about this wedding for a long time, and not only because we had to make a run for it when the rain started." The storm was nothing but a memory now, and the clouds were beginning to break. The air was cool and sweet, the only way it could after a storm that intense. It would be perfect for the elaborate fireworks display set to start later on after Ari's surprise guest arrived.

First, there was a matter of dinner, meaning we had to take our seats while fresh champagne was poured. The wedding party sat at a long table draped with floral garland and lined in candles and crystal from one end to the other. Once we were settled, I peered down the table and found Barrett standing with his champagne flute in hand. Somebody handed him a microphone which he tested before speaking. "This is around the time the best man tries not to make a fool out of himself," he began with a chuckle. "I promise not to embarrass either the groom or the bride. I promised my wife I would take it easy on the drinks until after my speech." He looked down at Lourde, who didn't bother pretending he wasn't telling the truth as she shrugged.

Once the laughter died down, he got serious. "There's something special about watching one of your best friends getting married. Ari, Magnus, Connor, and I have decades of friendship between us. We've seen each other through all of life's ups and downs, and I have no doubt we'll continue doing so for the rest of our lives. I'm that sure of my friends. They'll be there for me just like I will for them. The way we always have been."

He looked down the length of the table, and his gaze softened. "The only difference is nowadays, we don't have to support each other alone. I don't have to worry about my friends because I know they've all found their true partners... their soulmates. That's not a word I would have used before finding my own. If you know me, you know how true that is," he added, and those of us at the head table could only laugh knowingly. "But it's true. Ari and Olivia were meant to be and one of those things that's written in the stars. They found each other when they needed each other most, and the same was true for the rest of us. I've had the pleasure of watching all of us become the men we were meant to be, thanks to the presence of the women we were meant to be with. Looking down this table, I couldn't be prouder to be part of this group. Here's to many more celebrations like this one. Here's to many years of love and happiness for Ari and his beautiful bride, Olivia."

I couldn't have said it better myself. We all had found our true center after years of searching for what we never knew we were missing. With these women by our sides, there was nothing we couldn't do.

When Barrett raised his glass, we all did the same, toasting the happy couple and the many years ahead. "Now," he concluded with a grin, "... let's eat so we can get the party started."

11

MAGNUS

There were worse ways to wake up than with a mouth wrapped around my dick.

A knowing smile stirred my lips as I became aware of Evelyn's lips moving up and down my shaft. Her tongue lapped at the underside before flicking the bundle of nerves beneath my head. I gently moved my hips, working my way deeper until I hit the back of her throat. "Good morning to you, too," I muttered, opening my eyes and lifting my head to watch her work me.

Fuck, there was nothing sexier in the world. So many women complained about giving head, but my wife enjoyed it. Because she enjoyed it, not to mention wanting to satisfy me, she put her all into it. That only made it better, the way she let herself go and gave herself over to the process of giving and sharing pleasure.

Her low moan sent vibrations running through me, and I closed my eyes again, succumbing to the sensations racing through my body. I couldn't help but reach down to cup the back of her head, burying my fingers in her hair. "You're so good to me," I groaned out while she bobbed up and down, slurping on me. Her hands ran over my abs and chest, adding to the sizzling pleasure that began to build in my core. There was only one place I would rather have my dick than in her expert mouth. Knowing my wife, she'd be good and wet by the time she finished.

She increased the pressure, her cheeks hollowing out. It was too much to stand. While it would've been easy to let go and fill her throat, I pulled her away. "Why don't you climb on me and let me put that pussy to work?" I grunted, pulling the covers back so I wouldn't miss anything. I wanted to see every inch of her as she lost herself.

She gave me a seductive smile as she worked her way up to her knees. Her body glowed in the morning sunlight streaming through the windows at her back, highlighting every soft curve. She was an angel. Only there was nothing particularly holy about the way she straddled me and wasted no time running my swollen head through her folds. "I thought you'd never ask," she whispered.

Sure enough, she was dripping wet. What had I done to deserve a woman who got off on giving me head? Whatever it was, I planned on continuing to do it for the rest of my life because there was nothing better than this.

Once I was thoroughly coated in her hot, ambrosial juice, she guided me to her entrance. We both lost our breath as she slowly descended. All the while, she watched me, her eyes trained on my face while I indulged in the firm softness of her tits. "You are so goddamn beautiful," I told her once she took all of me inside her, settling at my base.

Her lips stretched in a smile as she leaned down to kiss me, rocking her hips in time with every slow, sensual thrust of her tongue against mine. With her dark hair hanging in loose waves on either side of my face and her body wrapped around mine, she was the only thing in my world at that moment. It was only the two of us lost in each other.

She broke the kiss with a gasp, bracing herself with one hand on either side of my head and arching her back, thrusting her tits close to my face. I took advantage, kissing, fondling, licking, and sucking, driving her wild the way she drove me crazy with every deliberate stroke.

"Make yourself come for me," I growled out, running my hand down her sides until I took her hips and pressed my fingers against her soft flesh. I knew her by heart but never got tired of every inch of her. She was an endless source of pleasure.

Especially when she let herself go the way she did now, chasing her high, single-minded in her purpose. There was nothing for me to do but grit my teeth and hang on for her sake. She had already worked me up until it was sheer willpower keeping me from exploding. Not yet. Not until she got hers.

I slid a thumb between us and found her clit. Her mouth fell open before a cry filled the room. "Oh God, yes." She gasped when I began tracing circles over the sensitive bundle of nerves, soaking in every helpless moan that tumbled from her lips.

"Come for me," I urged, jerking my hips upward to meet her stroke for stroke. "Let me see you come, baby. Let me feel it." Her muscles tightened, almost like they were responding to my whispered words. Maybe they were.

Soon, the bed creaked in time with every desperate, deliberate thrust. "So close," she whispered hoarsely, closing her eyes and screwing up her face in concentration. "Almost there."

"I want you to drench me," I muttered, stroking her clit faster, fucking her as she fucked me, using her as she used my body for her pleasure, knowing there was nothing but love between us. "I want your cum running down my balls by the time you're finished. Can you do that for me? Can you be a good girl and come that hard?"

That was what did it, the way I knew it would. It pushed her over the edge, giving me the thrill of watching a look of pure ecstasy wash over her flushed face. She was barely able to bite back a scream before crashing against me, her cunt milking my cock until there was no choice but to fill her. I came until my ears rang, and I couldn't breathe. It didn't help that Evelyn fell against me in the aftermath of her release, forcing the rest of the air from my lungs.

We were both breathless and a little sweaty. And very happy. At least, I was. I couldn't speak for her, though the dazed smile she wore when she finally managed to roll away told me she was feeling pretty good.

Only one question played at the forefront of my thoughts now that bliss had wiped everything else away. "What did I do to deserve that?" I was still a bit dazed, though I was not complaining.

"I woke up, and there was this big, gorgeous erection waiting for me," she explained as if it was the most obvious thing in the world. "How was I supposed to resist?" She giggled as she rolled my way, curling her body around mine.

"I thought it was because weddings get you frisky," I whispered, stroking her hair when she rested her head on my chest. "It's good to know all it took was the sight of my cock."

"The wedding might've had something to do with it, too," she replied. "It was a beautiful day."

And a beautiful night. The party had lasted until well past midnight, with the last of us retreating to our rooms around two in the morning. Reilly Kissinger had long since finished performing, and the band looked like they were ready to drop, but that was nothing compared to the weary but happy guests who managed to close the party down, us included.

"Everything was perfect," Evelyn decided with a smile. "And Olivia was so thrilled when Reilly arrived. It was the perfect surprise."

"So she was really surprised? She didn't have the slightest idea?" I found it hard to believe, but then Ari had made a big deal of swearing everyone to secrecy.

Evelyn snorted. "You heard the way she screamed when that helicopter landed." I had to laugh because yes, I had heard her scream. It was enough to worry me a little, in fact. "It was perfect. Something out of a fairy tale."

"Ari and Olivia got their happily ever after," I agreed, and I wasn't being sarcastic.

She was smiling sweetly when she lifted her head to gaze up at me. "We all did. Every one of us."

There was nothing to do but kiss her after something like that, so I did. It was the sort of kiss that deepened quickly and had the potential to lead somewhere else if it hadn't been for the knock at the door.

Right away, Evelyn jumped up and grabbed for the silk bathrobe she'd left across the foot of the bed. "Just a minute!" she called out while I sat up and arranged the blankets around my waist. I loved watching her excitement at being with the girls, and I couldn't pretend it didn't thrill me a little too. I loved seeing them, loved being with them. From the time they were born when their pediatrician told us we were the only two parents in the entire world who weren't satisfied by their babies sleeping well, there was no staying away from them. From the very beginning, we strug-gled with never wanting to put them down.

Evelyn opened the door so the girls' nanny could bring them into the room. "They had their breakfast," Penny announced as Valentina and Aria toddled in, wearing matching pink dresses. Both reached for Evelyn as soon as they set eyes on her, their pudgy little hands opening and closing.

"Thank you so much," Evelyn told her, a baby balanced in both arms as she returned to the bed. "We'll be getting ready to go down for breakfast soon, ourselves. I'll let you know."

"There's my girls," I called out as they approached the bed, and their sweet squeals made my heart swell. They shared delicate, dark curls and eyes the same shade of blue as mine, eyes that danced with joy once Evelyn set them down on the bed. They wasted no time crawling all over me, then over Evelyn once she climbed in next to me.

We spent time laughing and cuddling, and as we did, I couldn't help but remember the way the morning after a party used to go back in my single days. I would inevitably wake up beside a nameless stranger, and the first question on my mind was always how to get her out of my apartment without making things awkward. It always went that way, no matter how hot I'd been for the girl hours earlier. I couldn't be bothered to spend another minute with them.

This was better, spending some alone time with my reasons for existing. I couldn't imagine a time when I wouldn't be grateful for that or them.

The three girls who had turned me into a man.

12

MAGNUS

There was nothing like the morning after a big party. It meant seeing people at their most real. The guests Ari and Olivia had invited to spend the night—close friends, family, their inner circle—looked bleary-eyed and exhausted as they filed into the mansion's formal dining room, which had been cleared of its massive table and antique chairs in favor of smaller, round tables brought in for this morning.

The welcome aroma of strong coffee cut through what was left of the haze I was floating in. Time spent in bed with Evelyn, followed by cuddling and playing with the twins, hadn't been enough to fully wake me.

A lavish buffet was set up along one wall, featuring nearly every breakfast food known to man. There was also a Belgian waffle station, freshly made omelets, and a carving station featuring ham and prime rib. "Remind me to throw a big party sometime soon," I murmured to Evelyn while I scanned the room, searching for any of our group who might have wandered down by now.

"Admit it," she joked, nudging me while wearing a

playful grin I found irresistible. "You're a sucker for a good buffet, that's all."

"And an open bar," I added. "Don't forget an open bar."

"What was that about an open bar?" Connor asked, falling in place beside me with Pepper's hand in his. "I'm always up for an open bar, especially when I'm hung over. I need something strong, pronto."

"That's the thing about being settled down," Pepper observed, winking at Evelyn. "They aren't used to partying the way they did back in the day."

"Excuse me?" Connor countered with a snort. "I'm the guy who got caught by paparazzi dancing on a table in Vegas not long after we tied the knot. There is photographic evidence of a bartender mixing drinks in my mouth mere days ago." He sounded proud of himself.

"Shit, I forgot to check and see if the pictures went live," I admitted.

"Let's just say I woke up to no fewer than a dozen angry texts from the old man," Connor told me, rolling his eyes. "He knows there's nothing he can do about it. It's not his company to... how did he put it? Run into the ground?"

"It was also a hell of a way for him to find out he has a daughter-in-law," I pointed out as we got in line for the buffet. "I'm assuming you hadn't told them yet."

"We were hoping to make it a little more personal than a phone call," Pepper explained. "And honestly, it's not easy to get his mom and dad in the same room. They're always off doing their own thing separately." Another reminder of the man I did not want to be.

"Good morning." Lourde cut between Connor and me, tapping her brother on the shoulder. "How many texts did you get this morning?"

"Twelve," he replied, and the fucker managed to sound sort of smug about it. "How many did you get?"

"Fifteen," she crowed. "From both Mom and Dad."

Connor scoffed. "That doesn't count. All of my texts came from Dad. I still win." They burst out laughing before he added, "I wonder what first prize would be in that contest."

We were taking our seats at an empty table when a smattering of applause drew our attention to the doorway, where Olivia and Ari were entering the room hand-in-hand. "Good morning," Ari called out. "I hope everybody's enjoying their breakfast."

Connor snorted before smirking at me. "It looks like those two were busy enjoying other things all night." He had a point. I had never seen Ari look so exhausted, down to the circles under his eyes. But he was smiling, and anybody with working eyes could see the little looks he and Olivia exchanged as they made conversation with a few family members seated at another table. They may have been together for years and shared a child, but there was nothing like being newlyweds.

"We have to schedule a playdate soon," Lourde suggested to Evelyn. "Colton needs a little more time with his cousins."

"We'll work something out," Evelyn promised. "Shoot me a few good dates and times, and we'll go from there."

"I wonder if they'll be close as they grow up," I pondered as I cut into a fresh waffle loaded with berries. "Built-in friends, you know? I hope that's how it is."

"There's one thing we absolutely can't do," Lourde insisted, and now she looked serious. Turning to Connor, she said, "Remember how Mom and Dad always sort of unconsciously pitted us against other kids in the family around our age?"

"Unconsciously?" he asked with a sharp laugh. "It was completely conscious. Everything they did, we had to do better. Everything we did had to be better than something they had already achieved. Let's make sure we never do that with our kids."

"Our kids?" Evelyn asked, propping her chin on her hand before her gaze swung from Connor to Pepper. "Is there something you aren't telling us?" she teased.

Pepper's narrowed eyes and pursed lips made everybody laugh. "Hush your mouth," she warned. "Everything in due time."

Our table was complete once the bride and groom joined us. "How's everybody feeling this morning?" Ari asked after flopping into his chair.

"Better than you look," I replied. "Did somebody run you over after the reception?"

He shot me a withering look. "Don't pretend you forgot how it felt once everything was over and all the stress was gone. Don't get me wrong, I'm glad everything went off without a hitch, even with the rain. But it's going to take me a minute to recuperate."

"That's what a honeymoon is for," Olivia reminded him with a peck on the cheek. "This time tomorrow, we will be on our way."

"I'm serious." Lourde paired her words with a scowl, telling me she meant business. "If I so much as get a hint that you've opened your email while you're on this trip, I will boil you alive when you get back."

"Such violence," Connor whispered, wincing at his sister's threat. "I thought marriage and motherhood were supposed to mellow a woman out."

"I'm going to pretend I didn't hear that," she continued, pointedly avoiding looking at Connor in favor of staring at Olivia. "No work while you're away. I have everything under control."

Ari turned in his chair, lifting his eyebrows as he looked at his wife. "Did you hear that? Everything is under control. All you have to do is focus on having fun while we're away."

"I know, I know. But you know how I am," she grumbled. "I love to work. Is that a crime?"

"No, but it would be a crime to waste a beautiful honeymoon on work," Evelyn pointed out.

I shouldn't have chuckled, but I couldn't help it. "Says the workaholic," I joked, then flinched when she gave me a dirty look.

"I'm giving advice because I understand how hard it is to turn off your brain sometimes." Narrowing her eyes, Evelyn looked me up and down before snorting. "Clearly, not something you ever have trouble with."

Her little quip left everyone laughing, but not me. I was too busy fighting the impulse to drag her out of the room and go for round two in a darkened corner or closet somewhere. It wasn't such a mystery, really, since her snarky, even bitchy, attitude was part of what first drew me to her. The fact that she never hesitated to call me on my bullshit or to deflate my ego a little. I wasn't a hypocrite. I could admit there were times it needed deflating.

Barrett flagged down a server and asked for a screwdriver. He'd been strangely quiet through all of this, barely mustering a soft laugh or a grunt. "Do you plan on taking the table apart?" Connor asked, feigning ignorance when Barrett was clearly referring to the drink.

Barrett rolled his eyes. "So I went a little heavy on the

drinks last night. Nothing like the hair of the dog… I hope," he added, sounding miserable.

"Eat something greasy," Pepper advised, nodding sagely. "That's always the best cure."

"I can't remember the last time I drank enough to end up with a hangover," Barrett muttered, rubbing his temples. "I didn't think I drank too much, that's the thing."

"Do you want to be the one to tell him, or should I?" I asked Connor, who laughed in understanding.

"Tell me what?" Barrett muttered, eyeing me warily.

I took way too much satisfaction in folding my arms on the edge of the table and leaning in. "News flash, old man. It doesn't take nearly as much once you start getting up there in years."

"He just called you an old man," Lourde reminded him, clicking her tongue while laughter danced in her sparkling eyes. "Are you going to take that lying down?"

"Considering my head's about to split open, I don't think I have much choice." Even in his misery, Barrett could laugh at himself. "He's right. We're not kids anymore. We can't do everything we used to do."

Evelyn cleared her throat, raising an eyebrow at her brother. "From what I've heard, it's not a bad thing you can't do that sort of stuff anymore."

"All right, fine," he retorted. "I get the point. I'm a reformed man, which you well know." I was fairly sure he would kiss the girl who brought him his drink, which he barely stopped short of gulping.

Life was changing. There was no way of getting around it. I had to believe it was changing for the better, and we all had exactly what we needed. And as the years went on, as our lives continued to change and grow, we would still be there for each other. I was sure of it.

While she was at the table, the server asked, "Can I get anything for anyone else?"

"A bellini, please," Pepper requested, with Evelyn and Olivia nodding enthusiastically and asking for their own. I ordered another coffee while Ari and Connor followed Barrett's example.

Pepper stared at Lourde, tipping her head to the side. "Nothing for you?" she asked with a frown. "You feeling okay?"

Lourde's cheeks reddened before she exchanged a glance with Barrett, who nodded. "Might as well." He sighed before gulping down more of his drink.

"Might as well what?" Evelyn asked. "What don't we know?"

Olivia gasped. "Tell me it has something to do with you sending Naomi down to the drugstore in the village yesterday."

"You did that?" Evelyn's mouth fell open. "I didn't notice. Wait. Are you..."

Connor's eyebrows jumped up. "Are you?" he asked as a smile began to form.

Lourde spread her arms in a shrug. "I sent Naomi out for a pregnancy test, and yes. It came back positive. We're giving Colton a brother or sister."

"And you didn't tell us?" Olivia shrieked. She even threw her napkin across the table, which Lourde deftly caught. "How could you?"

"And steal attention from you on your wedding day? I hope you know me better than that." Lourde laughed through her happy tears as we congratulated her and Barrett, our voices overlapping. The group was about to grow again, and I could only imagine it getting bigger as time went on.

I exchanged looks with my best friends and knew they were thinking along the same lines I was. None of us could have predicted life would turn out this way, and we wouldn't have changed a damn thing.

EPILOGUE

LOURDE

Sixteen years later.

My favorite part of a big party came after the last guests had left, though I would never admit that to anyone else. It wasn't that I didn't want to be with them, and I didn't rush them out. It was more a matter of enjoying the silence that fell over our home in the aftermath of so much life and celebration.

If anything deserved a celebration, it was Colton's eighteenth birthday. How had eighteen years melted away in the blink of an eye? It was a question that had weighed on my mind for weeks leading up to the big event. My baby was now a man, just as handsome and cocky as his father but with just as big a heart too. I was proud of the person he had become and was still becoming, and it was clear from the sheer number of friends who had attended the party that he was adored. It was easy to love him, just as it was easy to love Barrett.

Barrett was now entertaining the rest of the hunk holes in his study. Years ago, he had taken down the wall between it and the next room, expanding the space until it was more like a man cave. There was a pool table, a few old-fashioned arcade games, and a huge television with a sound system that could rattle the entire penthouse when he cranked up the volume on a particularly loud movie.

I heard them in there as I passed the closed door and smiled to myself at their laughter. All these years, and they were still as close as ever.

On the other hand, the girls had decided to turn in after we'd spent an hour or two chatting in the kitchen over a few leftover desserts and a couple of half-empty bottles of wine. There was something profound about friendships like ours that had spanned decades. We had been together through all of life's ups and downs—our weddings, the births of our children, and even a few losses that had come along.

Ari's beloved grandmother came to mind. His daughter, Rose, had inherited Farrah's no-nonsense attitude and her keen work ethic, and she was only fifteen. I had never known a fifteen-year-old with so much drive, including my daughter. Farrah would've been proud of her.

The kids shared separate rooms from their parents, with Valentina, Aria, and Rose bunking with my Sienna. She and Rose were only a couple of months apart in age, thanks to Rose's conception falling sometime around her parents' wedding when I'd announced my pregnancy. The girls were like sisters, almost as close as Valentina and Aria.

The boys had retreated to Colton's room, where I lingered close to the door but heard nothing coming from inside. No doubt Noah and Colton were playing a video game while wearing headphones, something I wouldn't complain about. My only request tonight was for the kids to stay in rather than the older ones going out to raise hell. They were still underage, though that didn't seem to make much of a difference to many of their classmates. The stories I heard were almost enough to make me consider investing in strong locks on their bedroom doors. I could only hope they managed to avoid the pitfalls of growing up in a fast-paced world.

I was about to finish my walk-through, turning out lights as I went before noise from the balcony beyond the living room caught my attention. At first, I assumed the boys were out there sneaking drinks, thinking they could get away with it the way kids their age always did. Every generation thought they invented being sneaky.

Instead of rushing out to startle them, I slipped off my slingback pumps and carried them with me, creeping on silent feet until I reached the slightly open door. I wasn't going to raise a fuss. I only wanted to startle them.

"I can think of one thing I didn't get tonight." I recognized Colton's voice, barely raised above a whisper. He was likely trying to talk Noah into doing something they both knew would be frowned upon.

A second voice answered him. "Colton, we shouldn't..."

The sound chilled my blood because the voice did not belong to a young man. It was a girl's voice, one I recognized after having heard it for fifteen years. I didn't want to believe it. I wasn't sure I wanted to see what was waiting on the terrace, but I could keep myself from taking one step after another.

By the time I stepped out into a balmy night high above the city, I found my son with his arms around none other than Rose Goldsmith. The lights I hadn't turned off in the living room cast just enough of a glow to let me see them kissing passionately. Rose's fingers ran through Colton's hair while he ran his hands over her back. It was obvious after a few moments of shocked silence that I needed to intrude.

"What do you think you're doing?" I demanded. At the sound of my outrage, they flew apart, both flushed and breathless.

"Mom." Colton looked at Rose, then at me. The poor girl was trembling, on the verge of tears, thanks to being discovered. "I can explain."

"Please, do," I urged, folding my arms. The quiet peace I'd enjoyed only moments earlier was gone, replaced by a sense of foreboding at my son's poor decision-making. "Please explain why I found you kissing a girl who's too young for you and may as well be your sister."

THE END.

HOLD ONTO THE ELITE MEN A LITTLE LONGER...

Announcing...

The Elite Heirs of Manhattan Series.
Coming July 2024.

Step into the world of the next generation—meet the adult children of the Elite Men.

Prepare for forbidden, steamy love stories that will keep you up late at night...

Preorder Book One SEDUCTIVE HEARTS today!

ELITE HEIRS OF MANHATTAN SERIES #1

SEDUCTIVE HEARTS

MISSY WALKER

CHAPTER ONE
COLTON

Very few things could ruin a night out with my closest friends.

A text from my father was one of them. Bonus points if he was good and pissed.

Dad: *Get your ass home. Now. My study.*

He was definitely good and pissed. It didn't matter that I had a home of my own, nor that I was in the middle of having drinks with the guys. The great Barrett Black had made a proclamation and expected the world to comply.

I settled back in my chair, staring at the message while holding a glass of scotch in my other hand. "Fuck me," I muttered before finishing off the rest of my drink, savoring the heat which spread through my chest. It was a lot more pleasant than the burning, seething heat Dad's constant scrutiny usually stirred up in me.

"Fuck you? No, thanks." My cousin, Lucian Diamond, laughed before lifting his hand to get our server's attention —a cute girl, if too perky for my taste, somebody who probably would never rub shoulders with people like us if it wasn't for her job. She knew it was in her best interest to smile brightly and be a little flirtatious, and she had given us plenty of both.

She flashed that blinding smile again when she joined us. Her gaze darted around the small corner table, taking us in one at a time—Lucian, Noah Goldsmith, my oldest friend, Evan, and me. Tipping her blonde head to the side, she asked, "Are you all brothers? I swear, you look so much alike!"

We did, somewhat—tall, dark-haired, athletic. Maybe the similarities appeared stronger in the bar's dim lighting, or perhaps she was kissing ass for a bigger tip by starting a conversation, getting personal. "Something like that," I settled for.

"Wow. What a gorgeous family." She shook her head like she couldn't believe it before asking, "What can I get you, boys?"

Noah had been my best friend practically since we were born, so it didn't come as a surprise when he leaned back in his chair and deliberately looked her up and down. "I don't know. Are *you* on the menu?" he asked before sharing the kind of grin that normally sent a woman's panties sliding to the floor.

"Don't listen to him." Evan shook his head and pretended to scowl at Noah. "He has no manners."

Lucian lifted his hand to regain the girl's attention. "I was going to order another round. How does that sound?" he asked, looking around the table.

"Not for me." I knew I would catch hell for it, but I refused the offer. "Gotta go take care of something."

"Or someone?" Evan asked, snickering once the server bounced away. He gazed at her retreating ass before grunting out, "Dibs on that one."

Noah knew me best and laughed knowingly. He

narrowed his eyes, looking me up and down as I patted my pockets to make sure I had everything. "No, not the way you're thinking," he predicted with a snicker, elbowing Evan to get his attention. "I know that look."

Shooting him a cold glare, I demanded, "What look?"

"The look that says your balls crawled up into your belly when you got that text from Barrett," he announced with a laugh. "Sorry. I could see the screen from here." The others laughed with him, which was no big surprise, while I quietly seethed.

"Go fuck yourself," I grumbled once they calmed down. Certain topics were off-limits as far as I was concerned, at least in public—no busting each other's balls about our demanding parents.

And in my case, disappointed parents. No, *parent*. Singular. There wasn't much I could do or say that would get my mom too upset. The few times I'd ever witnessed my parents arguing was over me and the fact that Dad thought she was too easy on me. More than once, he'd called me a spoiled brat. All because he'd worked to get where he was, while all I'd ever had to do was rely on him and my trust. It's not my fault I wasn't driven like he was, not having goals and ambitions and all that shit.

"He can't know about Veronica yet, can he?" Lucian's brows knitted together before he winced. "I mean, unless he got word from my dad." He winced again, almost like he felt guilty for his father making a phone call.

Yes, trouble seemed to find me again this evening, but then again, Veronica never could handle her liquor. To think her wild temper was one of the things that had drawn me to her in the first place. That and a killer pair of legs that went up to her neck and tits with the power to make me drool. I couldn't keep my dick from waking up a little at the memory.

But not for the first time did I ask myself what the point was of having a media empire in the family if stories about a good-for-nothing playboy having a public blowout with an internationally famous model couldn't be suppressed.

Would that be too much to ask?

A little family loyalty?

No, instead, our dads lived by their ancient bro code. Uncle Connor would have rather gone behind my back and rat me out to my old man than bail me out for once.

"I'll deal with it, either way," I told him, then lifted a hand before leaving the table and making my way to the exit. The bar was pretty damn close to packed, full of beautiful bodies, some of which I would've liked to get to know a little better. Instead, I settled for nodding at the blatant *come-hither* looks I received from one eager woman after another.

Something told me getting chewed out by my father wouldn't be nearly as pleasant as what I could get up to with one of these willing partners.

The night was warm but still cooler without so much body heat pressing in from all sides. After signaling the valet, I rechecked my phone. The text wasn't any more pleasant than it had been when I first read it, and my jaw ached thanks to my grinding teeth.

The arrogant asshole.

He snapped his fingers and expected me to come running.

If I was, it was only to spare Mom his ranting over me. She didn't deserve that. If he had something to say, he could tell it to my fucking face.

Earlier tonight, I broke up with a coke addict who would only end up causing further embarrassment, yet somehow, my father would find a way to make me the villain.

Once the car arrived and I tipped the valet, I slid behind the wheel and wrapped my hands around the leather. It was a satisfying feeling, something like regaining control after the shame I would be blamed for heaping on my family only hours ago. The Bugatti shot forward like a bullet from a gun, tearing through the night. I liked to drive fast. I didn't have time to waste, even when I had no doubt I'd get my ass handed to me once I arrived at my destination.

It had been years since I'd moved out of the penthouse my parents shared. Yet, pulling the car into the familiar parking garage felt like stepping back into the past. I moved on autopilot, parking in one of the family's designated spots. My parents' cars were present, along with the pair of black BMWs they used when they required a driver, the other reserved for my sister, Sienna. At least Dad hadn't called her in to witness my assassination.

I rolled my eyes and sighed as I exited the car and headed for the elevator. At least I'd had the presence of mind to stop home and change before meeting the guys, or else I would've reeked like the dirty martini Veronica had thrown at me before the fight had really heated up.

I was twenty-eight years old and well beyond the point of getting called into Dad's office for a talking-to. Yet there I was, staring at the light over the elevator doors and watching it change as I climbed. Once the final floor was illuminated, a soft ping preceded the doors sliding open.

It didn't come as a surprise to find Mom pacing the wide hall leading from the elevator to the living room. She was dressed in workout clothes, and I remembered she took some fitness class with my Aunt Evelyn a few nights a week.

Something told me it wasn't yoga or Pilates that had her looking flushed.

"There you are," Mom hissed, coming to a halt with her fists on her hips. "What were you thinking? I told you I didn't like that girl." She barely stopped short of shaking a finger at me as I approached.

"I had a feeling it was something to do with that," I murmured before groaning. "I can explain. You know I wouldn't do anything like that without a reason."

Mom held up both hands, shaking her head. "I don't want to hear it, and I don't need to. It's your father who wants to talk to you about this. He's waiting in his study," she said as if I needed to be told.

"What's the temper on a scale of one to ten?" I asked, arching an eyebrow as I turned my head to gaze down the hall leading from the living room deeper into the penthouse.

"Roughly fifteen," she whispered as her lips drew into a thin line. "And that's after I talked him down from level thirty. He's very, *very* upset. Don't say something you can't take back," she added in a frantic whisper as I began crossing the room.

"I hope you told *him* that," I muttered, squaring my shoulders as I walked. Now, I knew how a condemned man felt during that final walk down the tiled hall, heading toward certain doom.

Instead of striding through the partly open door all at once, I paused. Years of going toe-to-toe with the man had taught me a few things about how to best deal with him. The less I said, the better. I loosened my jaw and pulled in a deep breath, preparing myself to go blank-faced, if only to piss him off.

"Are you going to take all night out there?" Dad's voice

was loud and sharp. "Believe me, this won't get any easier for you if you keep me waiting."

The prick. I continued on and pushed the door open before striding into the familiar room. Instead of leaving it a single room devoted to work, Dad removed the wall between it and the room next door, turning it into more of a man cave. It had evolved over the years, but the old arcade games and pool tables were still in place. However, the home theater system had been greatly improved as technology advanced.

It was no surprise he wasn't in the mood to shoot a game of pool or screw around with his new VR headset. He sat behind his desk, a glass of scotch in hand, still dressed for work in one of his typical suits, though he had removed his tie and popped the top two buttons on his crisp shirt. After running a hand through his gray-flecked dark hair, he motioned for me to come closer. "I would ask if you would like a drink..." he began in a tight voice, "... but I understand you've already been on a tour of Manhattan's most popular night spots this evening."

I offered as much of a shrug as I felt like managing. "She came back from the bathroom with white powder around her nostrils. I reminded her that was a dealbreaker for me. She threw a drink in my face. It went downhill from there." With another shrug, I added, "Who knew there was a substance out there more addictive than I am?"

His inscrutable expression left me wondering whether he'd believe me. Probably not. It went against his nature. "Your Uncle Connor did me the favor of calling me to give me the heads-up. It will be front-and-center tomorrow morning across all social media platforms and online outlets," he growled out before spinning the computer so I could read the headline:

Son Of Manhattan Construction Billionaire In A Public Brawl With A Supermodel

"Not the family's proudest moment." He took a sip from his glass, eyeing me as he did. I was twenty-eight, too old for the sight of his disappointment to sting, but I had to fight off a flinch just the same. I couldn't remember a time he hadn't demanded more from me than I was able to give.

"The family will get over it." When I stepped toward one of the leather chairs in front of his desk, he cleared his throat loudly.

"I don't remember asking you to sit," he reminded me in a tight voice that felt a lot like a slap across the face. "And this little fiasco tonight wasn't the reason I wanted to see you. Though it's probably the perfect segue," he observed, staring into his tumbler and swirling what was left inside.

"What does that mean?" I dropped into the chair anyway and tried to ignore the way his voice had quieted to something closer to a slither. It raised countless red flags.

"I've let you get away with this for too long," he quietly mused, still observing his liquor in favor of looking at his son. "I told myself you would grow up and stop recklessly bedding and discarding women."

Staring at him while he sat in judgment of me for doing nothing more than what he'd done in his day was the straw that broke the camel's back. "I'm not giving up women for the sake of the family," I flatly informed him. "It's not going to happen."

"That's not an excuse for bumming around with no direction. No goals." Lowering his brow, he growled out, "Bedding every woman you brush up against doesn't count as a goal."

There wasn't much I hated more than hypocrisy. I knew damn well what a notorious reputation he had when he was my age. There was a reason Mom and her friends had a special nickname for the great Barrett Black and his crew. The hunk holes. I couldn't let it go. "It was for you at one point," I muttered.

"Watch it." I could barely see his eyes, they were so narrow. "I was still running the business at that point. I built it from the ground up. Yes, I played hard, but I worked twice as hard. You keep this up, and that trust fund of yours might just be revoked."

A shock wave rolled through me at the threat. Of all things, I never expected that. "You would cut me off?" I asked, stunned. I always knew he was a self-important prick, but this was a new low, even for him.

He shook his head firmly. "I would never cut you off. I would, however, restrict your access to the assets. There's a reason the trust is revocable versus irrevocable."

He had me by the balls. The worst part was he knew it. That smug little grin he wore as I processed this and searched my brain for any way out told me so.

I could either fall in line and do as I was told or be cut off. If not exactly cut off, as good as. When I tried to imagine living in some shitty studio apartment in Brooklyn, bile began to rise in my throat. I would have to start budgeting and buying groceries rather than going out for all my meals. I would have to live like a so-called normal person, and the idea repulsed me almost as much as the idea of working.

He sighed before placing the glass on the desk. "It's time to push you out of the nest and force you to fly. I only want the best for you, son."

I didn't like the sound of that. The back of my neck prickled, but I gritted my teeth to fight off any obvious reaction. "Meaning?"

A slow, taunting smile spread across his face. "You're going to work in the family business, and I've already set up your first project."

Fuck me.

CHAPTER TWO
ROSE

"He's going to be late." I rechecked my watch and frowned. We were supposed to meet at eleven thirty, and it was already 11:25. What a surprise. The spoiled little rich boy couldn't be bothered to show up on time.

"Pumpkin, relax. You have nothing to worry about." It was easy for my father to say that, sitting at his desk, completely secure in his position, not only with the company but in the world. He was settled and established. Me? I was stuck with no choice but to hand the most important project of my life so far to a man whose presence I couldn't stand. He was the symbol of everything I hated most about the spoiled little boys I had grown up around. The fact that I gave him my first kiss made me want to go back and strangle that version of myself. Then again, how could I have known?

It took experience to understand that there were selfish, irresponsible, lazy men who could also be charming and fun to hang around. I couldn't understand, back then, how toxic those men could be.

"I want this to go perfectly," I admitted to Dad as I slowly crossed his office. The biggest of them all, of course, was situated in the front corner of the floor. Manhattan stretched out stunningly on two sides of the room with floor-to-ceiling windows that used to almost scare me when I was little. I didn't like heights or being so close to the clouds.

Instead of admiring the view, I gazed up at the portrait of my great-grandmother Dad had hung in his office. They'd had a very special, close relationship. She was more of a mother to him than his mother ever was. It was only since Farrah's passing that the two of them had gotten a little closer, but at least five years had passed since I had seen my grandmother.

"What are you thinking?" Dad's voice was low, full of the fatherly affection he had shown me all my life.

I glanced his way over my shoulder before turning back to the portrait. The woman staring down at me was self-possessed. Almost regal. Impeccable. I recognized the curve of my own mouth in hers, and the steely blue eyes reflected back at me every day in the mirror. "I'm not really thinking," I admitted. "Sometimes, I like to look at her. She reminds me how far I could go if I really wanted to."

"Hell, I could tell you that much," Dad said with a laugh. "Just ask me. I'll tell you you could rule the world one day. You can do anything."

"Isn't that something all parents say to their kids?" I asked with a skeptical smirk, turning toward him.

"Maybe," he allowed with a dip of his chin. "But I mean it. I've known since you were a little girl that you could lead an army into battle if it came to that. Whatever you set your mind to, it's yours."

"Sure, but nobody lives in a vacuum, do they?" Folding

my arms, I pointed out, "We have to rely on other people to, you know, make it to a meeting on time."

His phone rang, and he picked up the receiver while holding up a finger. "Yes? Wonderful."

He checked his watch, smirking. "Send him right in," he said before hanging up and buttoning his navy suit jacket.

11:29. Colton Black liked to cut things close. My blood pressure was beginning to rise, and every thud of my heart against my ribs made my head throb. He was going to be the death of me, and we hadn't started work yet.

Relax. You can handle him. It didn't matter who he was. His past didn't matter, neither did ours. Not that we had a past.

Only one kiss.

The brief memory turned my blood to ice and made my stomach churn. I looked down at my suit and brushed off lint that probably wasn't there.

It had taken a solid hour to decide what to wear today before I'd spent another hour on my hair and makeup. I needed to be impeccable. I needed to set expectations from the jump.

I was in charge.

I knew what I was doing.

All he had to do was follow orders and keep the workers in line.

It was amazing. The things I could tell myself when I needed a little confidence. All that flew straight out the window the moment Dad's office door opened, and his assistant ushered Colton Black into the room.

When was the last time we had been in the same place?

A year, maybe more. Time wasn't enough to make me forget how gorgeous he was. Nothing short of complete amnesia would do that. His dark, almost swarthy good looks combined with an exceptional body and the graceful way he carried himself were enough to take my breath away in those first moments while he shook Dad's hand and they exchanged a few pleasant words. "Ari, so nice to see you."

There was something I had forgotten, though. Something that slammed into me in the most unpleasant way possible. How could I forget the way his deep voice affected me? Once I caught my breath, my pulse took off at breakneck speed. My palms went clammy. My nipples went hard. Saliva flooded my mouth, and I swallowed quickly before putting on something as close to a smile as I could manage. "Colton." I thrust a hand forward before remembering the clamminess.

It was too late for me to pull back.

Colton's much larger hand wrapped around mine, his forehead wrinkling, but that might have been a trick of the light. It was smooth again when he drawled, "Miss Rose Goldsmith. It's been too long." His rich voice was like velvet or maybe warm honey poured over me.

The telltale heat in my core only got hotter when he flashed a dazzling smile.

Get it together.

I withdrew my hand and resisted the childish impulse to wipe my palm on my skirt. Then, Dad asked us to sit in front of his desk. I settled in but was anything but comfortable, thanks to Colton's nearness.

It had been years since I was young and stupid enough to fall for him. Somehow, his being here after all that time passed hadn't changed a thing.

"There isn't much for us to discuss," Dad announced as he sat in his high-backed chair. He looked like the king of New York that way, sitting on top of everything while the city sprawled behind him. "I was hoping to go over the generalities before Rose walked you through the specifics. She can get you up to speed regarding our needs and timeline."

Dad looked my way, and I had to turn my attention from the cologne Colton was wearing. Whatever it was, it was almost enough to curl my toes. "Yes, I've arranged for lunch in my office," I explained with a brief but courteous smile.

"Wonderful. It would be nice to catch up a little too." Colton crossed one ankle over the other knee—the picture of comfort and confidence. How did he manage it? "Though I should tell you, Dad was generous enough to provide me with the files you already shared. I burned the midnight oil, acquainting myself with your needs."

My cheeks flushed when he looked my way. There couldn't be a double meaning behind his words. Could there? He wouldn't be that stupid. Then again, maybe I was giving him too much credit. I couldn't afford to make that mistake now more than ever.

"That's good to hear!" Dad was all smiles as he turned my way. "I knew this was the right choice. And we do like keeping things like this in the family, don't we? So to speak."

"You know the Goldsmiths are as close to the Black family as my Uncle Connor or Aunt Evelyn," Colton reminded him with all kinds of warmth and charm. Meanwhile, I sat there wondering whether ten years had changed the taste of his lips.

I shook it off in a hurry when he shone his warmth on me. "And Rose, here, is practically my sister."

"*She's practically your sister.*" He was screwing with me, using the words his mother had when she found us that night after his birthday party.

Until she'd come outside, it had been the most exciting, incredible moment of my life. The fulfillment of every naïve schoolgirl fantasy. Colton had been starring in them for years, ever since I was old enough to start noticing boys. Until then, he had been the only one I ever so much as looked at.

But then Lourde had found us. In the end, it didn't matter because before dawn the following morning, he'd already moved on to another girl. Some nameless nobody he'd been photographed groping in an after-hours club he'd been too young to visit.

I had cried for a week.

When I forced myself to meet his gaze, humor twinkled in his dark eyes. I wasn't going to flinch. I would not back down. "That must be why I keep getting the urge to give you noogies," I retorted with a sweet smile.

The slight widening of his eyes was more satisfying than any kiss could be. What, he thought I was going to sit back and let him taunt me on my home turf? Obviously, I had made a mistake and overplayed my hand at some point. He knew how I felt about him, or at least how my feelings had changed. He might have been a complete idiot, but he wasn't stupid. He'd noticed how I went out of my way to avoid him.

If he were waiting for me to crumble like a stale piece of cake in the face of his magnetism, he would be waiting a long time.

"Colton, we are so glad to be working with you." If my father had any hesitations about this, he did his best to hide them. Standing, he reached out to shake Colton's hand again. "I have nothing but faith in you, you know." Damn, if he didn't sound like he meant it too. I couldn't fathom how.

"Thank you, sir," Colton replied. "If only my father saw it like you do."

The men shared a knowing grin. They both understood

Barrett well. "He wouldn't assign you this project if he didn't know you could handle it. Besides..." Dad added, winking at me, "... Rose here will keep everything in line."

"I have no doubt." Colton looked my way and raised his brows in expectation. "Well? I'm in your hands," he offered.

If that were true, I would have to start using more sanitizer. Who knew where he had been? "I'll show you to my office," I offered as I stood. I hope sandwiches and salad will be all right for lunch."

Colton laughed. "Are you kidding? It will be the most nourishing meal I've had lately. It turns out the olives from a martini don't count as a serving of vegetables." Dad had to go and laugh at Colton's weak joke, which, of course, only encouraged him. I settled on leading the way out the door without bothering to wait for him to join me.

He would have to follow me.

He'd better hope he can keep up.

It was only when he fell in step behind me that I realized he was probably looking at my ass. I came within a heartbeat of swinging my hips before stopping myself. Things would be bad enough without me egging him on. The last thing I wanted was for him to think I was deliberately teasing.

"That's a nice suit," he murmured almost too softly. It was barely audible, but the meaning was obvious. That was all I was to him—someone to have fun with, like the empty-headed girls he usually preyed on. The ones who didn't bother looking beneath that gorgeous, perfectly put-together façade. If they ever had, they would have found nothing. Emptiness.

"So, how come I never see you around town?" he asked in a breezy, carefree tone as we entered my office. "I run into your twin cousins, Aria and Valentina, all the time."

Sliding his hands into the pockets of his slacks, he gave the room an approving look. "I even run into my sister sometimes," he continued, taking in the blown-up fashion sketches on the walls—vintage designs from the company's early days. "But never you. Don't tell me you've been avoiding me all this time."

Colton didn't get it. He still thought this was a big joke—an excuse to flirt, to exploit our longtime acquaintance. There wasn't a doubt in my mind that he figured he'd get off easy, thanks to that connection. He probably imagined he would coast by and take credit for the project's success. It was enough to make me boil.

"Let's get one thing straight." Folding my arms, I lifted my chin, staring at him head-on. I wouldn't give him an excuse to joke about me avoiding him ever again. That was a mistake, and I couldn't afford to make any with Colton Black. "We're not here to screw around, and I'm not charmed as easily as my dad. If you make another comment about my suit or anything else about me, I'll have you kicked off this project. Got it?" He was lucky I bit my tongue before threatening to kick him in the balls while I was at it. I was damn proud of my self-control, along with my strength. The wide-eyed teenager was long gone, and it was about time he figured it out.

I didn't expect him to cower.

I didn't expect him to roll over and show me his belly like a submissive puppy.

I also didn't expect the slow, knowing grin my warning inspired.

Somehow, I had flipped a switch, and all at once, the professional image dropped away to reveal the Colton I'd known was waiting all along. "Careful, now," he growled out, his flashing eyes moving up and down my body. "Maybe

I like it when a woman gets mouthy. You'd better stop getting me excited, or we won't be able to get any work done at all."

I should have ordered him out, called my father's office, and refused to go through with the arrangement. What did I do instead? I blushed to the roots of my hair and had to consciously keep my knees from shaking under the weight of his seductive stare. Much more of this, and I'd be begging him to take me on my desk—repeatedly.

He wouldn't make it easy to keep things professional.

If this were any indication, it would be downright impossible.

But come hell or high water, I *would* resist him.

Read on...

ALSO BY MISSY WALKER

<u>*ELITE HEIRS OF MANHATTAN SERIES*</u>

Seductive Hearts - Preorder now

Sweet Surrender - Coming 2024

Sinful Desires - Coming 2024

<u>*ELITE MAFIA OF NEW YORK SERIES*</u>

Cruel Lust*

Stolen Love

Finding Love

<u>*SLATER SIBLINGS SERIES*</u>

Hungry Heart

Chained Heart

Iron Heart

<u>*ELITE MEN OF MANHATTAN SERIES*</u>

Forbidden Lust*

Forbidden Love*

Lost Love

Missing Love

Guarded Love

Infinite Love Novella

<u>*SMALL TOWN DESIRES SERIES*</u>

Trusting the Rockstar

Trusting the Ex

Trusting the Player

*Forbidden Lust/Love are a duet and to be read in order.

*Cruel Lust is a trilogy and to be read in order

All other books are stand alones.

JOIN MISSY'S CLUB

Hear about exclusive book releases, teasers, discounts and book bundles before anyone else.

Sign up to Missy's newsletter here:
www.authormissywalker.com

Become part of Missy's Facebook Reader Group where we chat all things books, releases and of course fun giveaways!

https://www.facebook.com/groups/missywalkersbookbabes

ACKNOWLEDGMENTS

When I first wrote Forbidden Lust, I had no clue it would resonate with so many of you, nor did I anticipate Lourde and Barrett's popularity! Your embrace of the hunkholes and your enthusiasm for the story have been amazing. I'm thrilled to see the ideas in my head come to life and be enjoyed by all of you.

I couldn't have accomplished this without my brilliant editing team. Special thanks to my beta team: Karmin, Saskia, Maria, and Ella. Their invaluable input has truly made this possible.

Big shoutout to my editors who always push me beyond my limits. But you know I love you girls! A heartfelt thank you to Kay, Chantell, and Nicki for your incredible support and guidance.

And lastly, my fantastic 'Babes!' over in my Facebook reader group. To all the members of *Missy Walker Book Babes*, your humor always brings a smile to my face. I deeply appreciate diving into every comment and post you share, and I hold a special affection for the ever-growing community we've built together.

Much love,
Missy x

ABOUT THE AUTHOR

Missy is an Australian author who writes kissing books with equal parts angst and steam. Stories about billionaires, forbidden romance, and second chances roll around in her mind probably more than they ought to.

When she's not writing, she's taking care of her two daughters and doting husband and conjuring up her next saucy plot.

Inspired by the acreage she lives on, Missy regularly distracts herself by visiting her orchard, baking naughty but delicious foods, and socialising with her girl squad.

Then there's her overweight cat—Charlie, chickens, and border collie dog—Benji if she needed another excuse to pass the time.

If you like Missy Walker's books, consider leaving a review and following her here:

instagram.com/missywalkerauthor
facebook.com/AuthorMissyWalker
tiktok.com/@authormissywalker
amazon.com.au/Missy-Walker
bookbub.com/profile/missy-walker